The Middle of Elsewhere

Also by Alison Moore

Small Spaces between Emergencies
Synonym for Love

The Middle of Elsewhere

a novella and stories

Alison Moore

For Rosalyn From College Station to Dallas— I feel we've travelled far!

PHOENIX INTERNATIONAL, INC.
FAYETTEVILLE

© 2006 Alison Moore
Printed in the United States of America
ISBN-10: 0-9768007-1-3
ISBN-13: 978-0-9768007-1-2

Designed and produced by John Coghlan

"Miniature Graceland" won the Katherine Ann Porter Prize in Fiction and was published in the fall 2004 issue of *Nimrod.*

"Snake Woman" was published in *Story* magazine in a slightly different form.

"Angel of Vermont Street" was published in *Story* magazine and in *A Four Way Reader Anthology* in a slightly different form.

"Divided Highway" was published in the *Marlboro Review* in a slightly different form.

Library of Congress Cataloging-in-Publication Data

Moore, Alison, 1951–
 The middle of elsewhere : a novella and stories / Alison Moore.
  p. cm.
 ISBN 0-9768007-1-3 (alk. paper)
 I. Title.

PS3563.O568M53 2006
813'.54—dc22

2006010364

For Phil, fellow traveler

Contents

Acknowledgments

The Middle of Elsewhere is a place I've spent a lot of time in: Terlingua, Lamalara (Texas and Indonesia, respectively), as well as many detours in Far Left Field and Off the Beaten Track, both in exterior and interior ways. I'd like to thank my agent Ellen Levine, friend and editor Molly Giles, and Francine Ringold in particular. Special thanks also to The Writers Colony at Dairy Hollow, the Ucross Foundation and Mt. Sequoyah Conference and Retreat Center for the time and place to write. Gratitude goes out to family, both alive and otherwise. For my father, the self-proclaimed vagabond, who instilled in me the desire to be elsewhere, and to never forget what Robert Louis Stevenson once said, that "traveling hopefully is a better thing than to arrive."

The Middle of Elsewhere

Truth or Terlingua

Like a lost ship about to sail off the edge of the earth, a motor home that's seen better days rumbles out of Big Bend National Park. The man driving grips the steering wheel while his wife pores over a torn map of west Texas balanced on her knees. Their cat, Pity Sake, yowls unceasingly, wedged beneath the bucket seat. There should be a sign: *Abandon Hope All Ye Who Enter Here,* the admonition on ancient maps next to a drawing of a roiling sea serpent separating the known from the unknown world. But the only thing resembling signage is a bullet-shot piece of once-green metal saying Terlingua is five miles ahead.

Rooney looks through badly tinted glass at the community of Study Butte, its convenience store, marginal motel, the forlorn laundromat dwarfed by monumental, prehistoric cliffs and ominous volcanic outcroppings. Any minute now he expects to see dinosaur scat blocking the road. "Nothing but *rocks!*" he cries as if the landscape itself is a personal affront, a flat joke at the end of a cherished dream.

"It's a *desert,* Rooney. And I think it's absolutely wonderful." Francey looks at her husband cautiously. She doesn't really have the energy to humor him now. Contradiction is easier. Still, she softens a little. "It says in the book that the Comanche had a legend that the Creator brought all his leftover rocks here."

He looks out on the evidence of the Comanche legend. Leftover rocks. Extras. The rest of the world had taken the best and here's the dregs. He's been looking forward to getting here for several days; he'd seen a photograph of a waterfall in the Chisos Mountains in the *Lonely Planet* guidebook. But when they'd pulled

3

the motor home into Rio Grande Village RV Park two hours ago only to find all the hookups taken he felt frustrated, thwarted when the ranger told him he'd have to drive to a campground that wasn't even in the national park. Now that he's here with no water-fall in sight he's not even sure he wants to stay the night. Maybe they should turn around and go home. But where is that? Everything they own travels with them now.

"Is this still technically Big Bend? I expected something worth driving a thousand miles across Texas for," he says, his voice already lowering to a growl as if Texas itself, his native state that could eas-ily hold half a dozen other states quite comfortably, is deliberately thumbing its long, lone star nose at those who dare to drive to its edges. Especially like they just did, from Paris to Terlingua, from lush green ranchland all the way to Mars. They have yet to cross a single state line.

"It's only eight hundred and ninety-five miles," she says, "not a thousand." Correcting each other is a habit, a compulsive one, though she enjoys it, especially when she knows she's right and can back it up with footnotes; especially since Rooney tends to make pronouncements prefaced by "it's a well-known fact," or "studies have shown." Never in doubt, often wrong, that's what he is. Still, there's times when her heart goes out to him if he can admit error instead of taking a cheap shot in blame. And she needs her heart to go out to him now, not circling around like a bird whose flock has flown south without it. A new start, that's what they'd agreed on. Not détente.

Rooney takes the turnoff to Terlingua Ghost Town, reassured to see a working bank with an ATM and a post office with a flag at full mast. He's almost used to the way the motor home turns after taking out a couple of stop signs on the way home from the dealership in Paris. Thank God it was used, very used. Thank God he didn't get the Prowler or Predator or whatever it was called. The Intruder. Or worse, the Swinger. The larger model. He doesn't want to be lumped in with the snowbirds driving their big rigs down the interstates of the southwest. After all, he's only fifty-one and still a Liberal Democrat, even if AARP is flooding him with mail.

The Jamboree was the smallest thing on wheels he could find that he thought they could actually live in. He still considers himself a vagabond even though times have changed. Back in the sixties he drove a VW bus with a bad carberator out to the coast with a well-thumbed *Peoples' Guide to VW's* in hand. Now he's got AC, cruise control. But he drew the line there. No satellite dish. No senior citizen welder sunglasses. Not him.

"There it is," Francey says hopefully. "Big Bend Travel Park. Just like the ranger said." It's not inside the park boundary, even if it does call itself Big Bend, but at least there isn't a "campground full" sign out front.

Rooney steers slowly through the gate, looking for the office to register. There isn't one. Nor is there a campground host that he can see. Just a couple of scruffy dudes with beers and guitars sitting on stumps in front of an old aluminum Spartan trailer that looks as if it hasn't moved in years. He sidles up to them with the Jamboree, rolls down Francey's window so she can ask where to check in.

One of them, the one who stops strumming, says, "Just take any old site. There's envelopes in the bar—opens at five."

A black dog trots by with pink Mardi Gras beads around its neck, a chicken leg clamped firmly in its jaws. An enormous raven squawks malevolently from a power pole.

Rooney looks around. All he can see is a squat building, if you can call it a building, more like a cobbled-together bunker than a bar. A rustic sign in front of it says "La Kiva."

From what he can see, there aren't exactly campsites. Gray power hookup boxes stick up at odd places; there's a damp spot next to one that, hopefully, indicates the presence of potable water. Funky he can handle but this place looks as if it should be condemned.

Francey points to what seems to be an available space next to a sawed-off cottonwood stump. She gets out to inspect. No number. She shrugs and starts to wave her arms like those people in airports that guide planes into the gates. It's almost dusk and Rooney wishes she'd taken a flashlight. He peers into the rearview mirror, trying to back in. He isn't exactly sure where she is and she has a bad habit of standing right behind the Jamboree. He's never sure whether she means left or right and whether rearview mirrors reverse things. She does it on purpose, he's convinced, to make him look inept. It's easy to lose your bearings when you're trying to back up something the size of a bus. And it doesn't help any that he doesn't roll the window down so he can hear her instructions.

"Stop!" she shrieks. But he's just winged the picnic table, hears the sickening crunch of splintering wood. He slams on the brake anyway, then rolls forward again. "It's not too bad," she calls out. "It was already broken."

But he takes it hard, just the same, the broken table physical evidence now of other things breaking down, both inside and out. Defective parts have become a bane to his existence lately, and now he's arrived at a cul se sac in purgatory where he might be stranded indefinitely.

"Close enough," Francey says. And she's right. They've got half a mile of extension cord if they need it, five fathoms of hose.

He shuts down the Jamboree and climbs out. By the time his boots hit the ground Francey is already in the kitchen. He's starting to appreciate this new, old-fashioned division of labor, the pioneer protocol. She's in there rustling up the grub while he's stabling the ox, sizing up the other oxen, the Winnebagos and Hitchhikers. The Storm. Who names these things? Whatever for?

He pulls the extension cord from the hatch where it's coiled and stowed, plugs it in to the gray box tilting from a pile of rough concrete. The water spigot lies well hidden in a patch of dead weeds full of stickers, so close to the ground it's hard to get the hose connected to it. The gray water hose seems easier to push into its receptacle. He yells for Francey to turn everything on.

She yelps as air from the hose spits water into the sink. She laughs out loud. She can't remember the last time she did. It feels good in her belly, her mouth. She flips on the AC. Nothing. The microwave. Nada. Toaster oven. Coffee pot. All in rapid succession. Not a whimper from the appliances. But she can't stop laughing.

"You sure you plugged it in?" she says.

He could just kill her for saying that. Rooney eyes the gray box suspiciously, wanting to blame it. He's not sure of anything but he'll be damned if he'll admit this yet out loud. Then he sees the wires dangling.

He kicks the offending box.

Francey turns from the window above the sink. She doesn't want to see it, that infantile rage, that impotent lashing out against humiliation that men seem to need to do to get even. But women, she reminds herself, just implode; they wreak havoc on their insides, which is not necessarily a more effective strategy.

He looks across the way at another motor home, a really big one with Saskatchewan plates, and a very tall, very tanned Canadian comes out of it with a hair dryer in his hand.

"Try this," he says to Rooney. "It'll save some time." He smiles helpfully.

Rooney doesn't get it. Then he does. You walk around with the hair dryer to all the gray boxes to find one that works so you don't have to drive your rig around with your wife waving her arms like a windmill.

Rooney thanks the man. He walks the entire campground plugging in the hairdryer before he realizes that the Canadians—there are several enormous motor homes with Saskatchewan plates—three generations, from all appearances, all blond, are all traveling together. They've gotten all the available power. An unprecedented Canadian coup. And they're watching him.

He goes to return the hairdryer. The man shrugs good-naturedly. "That's Terlingua for you," he says.

"What does that mean?" Rooney asks uneasily. But he really wants to know.

The Canadian shrugs again. "From what I've read, it's a bad translation meaning 'three languages.' Spanish, English, Comanche, maybe."

Rooney is starting to realize he doesn't know much of anything. About motor homes or electricity or Terlingua. Or Canadians.

The Canadians have their extended family with them. An entourage. He and Francey are on their second cat, Pity Sake, a cousin to Pity Sing named after a cat in Flannery O'Connor's story "A Good Man Is Hard to Find." Francey dotes on it but Rooney can't help but look at the cat as a poor substitute for progeny.

Francey leans out the Jamboree door, trying to read Rooney's body language. He looks so small next to the man with the hair dryer, his fists balled up in his pockets. And his hair is thinning on the crown—from the top step of the Jamboree she has a bird's eye view of him that she normally doesn't have. He looks smaller than usual. His fists are clenched, his feet planted a foot apart. Where is the high school sweetheart, the champion pole vaulter that she fell in love with? She's not sure she should look too closely. He's changing. Into what, it's hard to say from here. A shadow of his former self? It's way too soon to tell.

"You could plug into ours—we only use 110 and there's still 220," a man behind him calls out. Rooney turns. There's a voice coming from a blue and white travel trailer with Route 66 decals all over it. From where Rooney stands, it looks like something the Jamboree hatched when he wasn't looking, an egg-shaped thing on wheels not more than ten feet long. A couple sits beneath a tiny awning strung with little lighted skulls. They're sipping coffee from Route 66 cups and grinning like fools.

"What kind of trailer is *that*?" Rooney asks, coming closer.

"It's called a Love Bug," the woman says. Her long hair curls over her breasts nearly covering a T-shirt sporting a smiling skeleton holding an artist's palette and a brush. "Art is Hell," it says, as if you have to be dead to stop denying it.

He wonders if she's kidding. Not about art being hell, but about what the trailer's called. Maybe it's what *she* calls it. But whatever it's called, they look happy in front of it watching the last of the sunset and the wall of crimson clouds building up behind it, all by themselves.

"That's the brand name, Love Bug," the man says, as if sensing the skepticism behind Rooney's raised eyebrows. His brown hair is windblown, hanging in his blue eyes. A respectable beginning to a beard. "They don't make 'em anymore. We got it on ebay."

Rooney notes the license plate on their pickup. Arkansas. Doesn't add up, somehow. They seem more San Francisco or Santa Fe than Little Rock. And who ever heard of a Love Bug? The only one he'd ever heard about was the VW PeeWee Herman drove. This is a trailer. He imagines them having hot sex in there, day and night for fun, not procreation. They look late thirty-ish, agile enough to accomplish complex positions even in something the size of a tiny Tuff-Shed.

A short, round woman in flowered Capri pants, Reboks, and an oversized, plain pink T-shirt approaches. She holds out a thick foil packet. Rooney wonders if it's weed. She looks Mexican. "That's Terlingua for you," the Canadian would probably say. It could mean a lot of things.

"Tamales," she says, smiling. "Two fifty for six."

"No. No thank you. Not today," Rooney says, slowly backing away.

"Why not today? Fresh! Tamales!" She holds out the foil package, coming after him.

"They're really good," the man with the Love Bug says. "Try some."

"Francey!" he calls out. He doesn't like dealing with people from other countries. He's afraid he won't be able to make himself understood. Like in the dreams he has over and over where he has something urgent to say and all that comes out is a desperate croak.

He pulls the orange extension cord out of the gray box and walks over to the Love Bug, which seems to need so much less of everything. 110 indeed! How economically correct! It probably runs on testosterone. The couple disappears inside. He expects to see the thing start rocking and bucking any minute.

Francey is buying not one but two packages of tamales.

He plugs in. The Jamboree actually trembles as the AC, the microwave, the coffeepot, and toaster oven all go on at once. Up pops the automatic antenna like a flag of a newly declared country. Useless now since he'd deliberately left the TV behind, given it to a neighbor back in Paris. Francey laughs and hugs the warm tamales to her breasts. The skeleton lights on the Love Bug flicker but hold steady.

The Canadians lift glasses of tawny whisky in breakable glasses. Do Canadians drink Canadian Club whiskey, Rooney wonders, or would that be tacky? He wants them to stop watching, stop noticing everything, these well-heeled neighbors to the north. He gives them a mock salute.

The Canadian Club puts down their glasses and they all get into a Suburban wagon with bicycles bolted to the top, the third generation driving, the other two in the back. Rooney wishes he had something like that to tow so he and Francey could scoot around town without the millstone of the Jamboree. He tries to imagine a son, driving, a tanned arm resting casually in the open window. A son with a great sense of direction, computer literacy, and a genuine capacity for fun. But no, he and Francey have a Vespa, got it at a yard sale and strapped it to the back of the Jamboree. It almost got stolen by a gang of teenagers outside Del Rio while they stopped to eat at a Waffle Hut. Rooney saw them and ran out to the parking lot. As soon as they saw him, they scattered. He almost wishes they had managed to steal it. It's one more thing to haul around and they can only go someplace one at a time.

And maybe that's the point. It's for the best. After all, they'll be with each other 24/7 from now on. He hasn't really thought it through. But he's damned if he's going to buy one of those golf carts. Buying an RV was bad enough.

At forty-four, Francey's biological clock is ringing, loudly, with no snooze alarm. It's ringing in Rooney's ears and he hears it all the time. Time's up and it's still going, like something in one of those battery commercials. What was it? Of course. A rabbit. The EverReady Rabbit. Wasn't that also the name of a dildo?

Francey goes inside, starts shutting down the appliances. She bangs around in the cupboards looking for something to go with the tamales. Stuffing? No. Ravioli? Maybe. Hamburger Helper? Why not? She can dump in a whole jar of salsa to jazz it up.

Rooney sits down on the broken picnic table by the cotton-wood stump. He watches the black dog with the pink beads root-ing in a pile of half-eaten buffalo wings by the overflowing dumpster on the other side of this so-called campground. The raven, still on the power pole, seems to be telling it where to look. Two sites over, near what must be the creek for there's still some living trees growing, a car with sub woofers throbs on its wheels. As Rooney watches, the tinted windows roll down. A cloud of something sweet escapes like steam. The music doubles in volume. Norteño, he's pretty sure, but he wouldn't swear to it. A man with Tom Cruise sunglasses gets out and leaves the door wide open as he goes inside his trailer. He has no intention whatsoever of turn-ing off the stereo.

A light goes on at La Kiva. A trapdoor creaks open. A few cars arrive as if on cue and several people disappear down the hatch that serves as an entryway.

"I'm going over there to see about paying," he calls out to Francey. He's not sure if she actually heard him over the accordions. She'll figure it out. Her radar is impeccable.

Rooney picks his way down concrete steps into a cave. He fol-lows a dark passageway until he finds a door and on the other side a large grotto yawns. Or does it growl? He expects to see stalagtites, trolls underneath the bar. Glasses and bottles line the bar and familiar neon beer signs glow seductively; a few people in a dark corner around a table stop talking and stare at him. A tall man with a gray beard and hair, both down to his waist, wipes the bar with a rag.

"Early bird," he says to Rooney. "It's a good hour until open mic."

"I'm looking for an envelope," Rooney says.

"Was someone supposed to leave it here for you?" the bartender asks.

"I'm trying to pay for the camping!" Rooney says, exasperated now.

"Are you leaving?"

"No! I just got here!"

"Then don't worry about it. Have a beer."

"Well, if this is Terlingua for you, then I'm all for it," Rooney says with as much irony as he can muster. Now it's the bartender's turn to be pissed off.

But he isn't. "What'll you have?" he asks.

"Diet Coke," Rooney says, then changes it to a Corona. He's on vacation now. A permanent one.

He slides onto a stool. The bartender pushes a bottle toward him with a wedge of lime jammed into the neck. Rooney pulls out the lime and sets it on the bar, sips the Corona. It's been awhile.

A woman with grayish hair and a definitely red guitar case emerges from the dark passageway. "Hey, Mike!" she calls to the bartender. She's wearing blue harem pants with tiny brass bells stitched along the sides. Gold flip flops. A midriff T-shirt of an indefinite color over a very tan, very flat midriff. The guitar case is plastered with overlapping stickers. One in particular catches Rooney's attention. "Bush is a Punk-Ass Chump."

"Jesus Christ," he says, "where'd you get that?"

"Here," she says. "Isn't it great?"

He doesn't know what to say. It's outrageous. Maybe even dangerous. You could get shot in most parts of Texas displaying such a sentiment. Rooney can't help it. He smirks. He can easily imagine putting one of those stickers on the Jamboree. Another Corona and he'll seriously consider it. The country's in the crapper, after all, with the Bush mob at the wheel. Still.

"Saw Burro Judy today," the woman says to the bartender, "just past Miss Tracey's."

"Where's she going now?" Mike asks.

"Boquillas."

"She won't get back in."

"Maybe she's had enough."

Rooney has a vague recollection of reading something on moveon.org about border closings since 9-11, places where you used to be able to just walk across, buy lunch and souvenirs, and come back. Now every Mexican is a potential enemy. And maybe Terlingua is some hotbed of political anarchy in the eyes of Homeland Security. Outlaws from south Austin. Psych ward runaways from Big Spring. Two-bit terrorists from Waco with a pipe bomb and a web site.

The woman opens the guitar case, the latches snapping. Inside, a small Gibson with a jagged hole rests, perfectly still, like someone laid out for a funeral.

"My boyfriend shot it," she says to Rooney when she catches him looking.

"Holy shit," he says. He grins. She actually smiles back. He could start to like it here. "What'd he shoot it for?"

She looks at him like she's never considered the question. "I didn't stop to ask," she says. "He shot the guitar and then went to shoot the mirror in the telescope at McDonald Observatory where he used to work."

"Did he actually shoot it?" Rooney asks, impressed with the magnitude of this man's resentment, his spectacular revenge.

"Yeah. It's part of the tour now. But the bullets didn't break it. He was going after it with a pickaxe when they grabbed him and dragged him off to Big Spring. I guess I got off easy with the guitar, considering."

Rooney orders another. With a Cuervo Gold shot this time. When in Rome. One needs fortification here, obviously. He wonders where Francey is, what she's doing. He wonders if she wonders what he's doing, where he is, why it's taking him so long to find the envelopes. He feels like he's in a submarine and she's floating up there in a tanker. Damn the torpedoes anyway. They can live without each other for half an hour, surely.

The couple from the Love Bug walks in, lugging six instruments between them. Where do they sleep, with so much to haul around? They smile at Rooney. They look rested, happy, not worried that it'll probably take them an hour to tune everything.

Mike puts the PA together. Rooney wonders if he needs one of those hair dryers to check the plugs before he even bothers setting up microphones. Even the pay phone on the wall has an Out of Order sign on it. But the tap on the keg seems to be working just fine. Shiner Bock is flowing.

It's all flowing now. The trip here over hill and dale, down through piney woods of east Texas, giving way to the muggy flats of Houston, and all the fast lanes on Superbowl Sunday slowed down to a crawl. Eighty miles in six hours, a record, and Francey freaking out looking for NPR to drown out their howling cat in the dead zone halfway to San Antonio and all you could hear was Jesus this and the Lord said that. She sighed with relief when she found a station with acoustic guitar music until the chorus came around and they knew they'd been tricked again into listening to Christian music, where the kind of love being sung about had nothing to do with lust and longing and groping in the dark. By Del Rio they were resigned to it, just kept it on low volume. Rooney knew he should have bought the model with the CD player. They could have been listening to Kinky Friedman and the Texas Jewboys instead, someone who'd made an honest living out of being outrageous.

The Texas they knew, had been born in, courted in, settled down forever in, just flat disappeared after Del Rio. They could have crossed over into Mexico without realizing it, for all they knew. Trees disappeared altogether. Things looked desperate. Shot-up trailers. Skinny dogs skulking around burned-out cafes. Tumbleweeds the size of sputniks rolling across a desolate terrain he knew all too well in an interior way, now everywhere, out there, surrounding him. But behold! The first camping sign they found after dark was definitely that predictable shade of state-park brown. Seminole Canyon. They followed a winding road south toward a distant ranch light. And lo, there was the Texas flag on the squat brown hut and a nice note from the ranger telling which sites were still open: all of them. They crept into slot thirty-six on a scrubby, windblown mesa, and all night the wind pounded the Jamboree. Coyotes yowled and quarreled near the trash bin. Bats swooped around the light by the restrooms. Rooney didn't dare get out and plug in. Nearly ran the battery down instead as they huddled by the light of the microwave. The cat still had reliable instincts and hid in a cupboard under the sink and finally shut up when it was shut in.

But for all that, there was something almost intimate about it, a closeness they'd never really had in their cluttered but barren house. The elements were all around them and they were with each other, child or no child, and that was enough. He thought about what might be required of him in this new, more minimal life; he wondered if he could rise to the occasion. Francey didn't seem as worried. She closed her eyes and actually smiled. They didn't say much, just listened to west Texas, the wild they'd gotten themselves into thrashing around outside.

In the morning they left without paying. After all, they hadn't plugged in. Onward they went, westward toward Marathon.

They're on the road again, not only trying to outrun several failures, but trying to catch up, getting back to where they once belonged. They'd spent way too long in a house and got out just in time. The neighborhood they lived in rose and fell in market value. Mexicans moved in with their restaurants and *tiendas*, their lavish *quincinieras* and roadside shrines; Rooney now knew a few words of navigational Spanish. "*No aceptámos tarjetas de crédito,*" he learned from a sign at a taco stand; it came in handy when he had a yard sale. But he didn't really know much about the people themselves, how many had been downsized for no good reason, disenfranchised already by the broken promises of NAFTA, the *maquilladores* closing, their jobs going to Jakarta. Failure was everywhere to behold, it was all a matter of degree.

Francey said she was finally going to try to learn Spanish and had taped up Loteria cards on the dashboard of the Jamboree. She liked learning how to talk all over again. *El Borracho.* A man reeling with a bottle. *La Sandia.* Watermelon. *La Luna.* Moon, the face of a lovely, lonely woman in its crescent. *El Corazon.* Heart. The picture of the heart was luridly, anatomically correct, not the stylized, sterilized valentine kind. It had valves and arteries and veins as if it had been cut out of a cadaver and was ready to be transplanted into someone who wouldn't live much longer without it.

They hadn't been on the road long enough to know where they'd put things when they'd packed. By the light of day he secretly watched her for signs of early Alzheimers. She was probably doing the same with him. Selective dementia would be a blessing, though; there are some things he'd rather not recall.

This getaway, for that's what it is since they had yet to come up with something they are actually going toward, could be traced back to a single phone call from the doctor at the fertility clinic. Not the nurse. The doctor. The call came two weeks after the implant of the egg in Francey's womb, an egg sequestered in a petri dish for *in vitro* fertilization. "I'm sorry," the doctor said. Rooney couldn't remember this one's name. "You're not pregnant." Francey was on the extension in the bedroom but it seemed the doctor was talking to him. He could hear her breathing, that's all. Neither of them could speak. The doctor said he was sorry again, asked them to think about their next step, but to give it time. Rooney hung up the phone, went back to the bedroom. Francey was still holding the phone to her ear, listening to dial tone. He had to take the phone from her, and she held on like she'd fight him to the death for it. She finally let go, looked up at him, and began to cry. Really cry. And it killed him, that face full of pain that he could do nothing about.

Their defeat was enormous. They'd made the rounds, run into the same couples nervously thumbing the magazines in the waiting room. They were a nomadic herd, the infertile, and they encountered each other in the tiny oases of the clinics, the ones that seemed to offer water to those dying of thirst. Rooney looked surreptitiously at the other potential fathers as they were summoned by the nurse into the little rooms with the headphones and the dirty magazines and the videos selected to ensure maximum ejaculation. Who chose these, the doctors? Or the nurses? Did they try them out, these videos, themselves? Rating the moaning, the penetration, the elaborate, mutual orgasms for their patients on a scale of one to five?

His sperm had "low motility," the last doctor said. Rooney pictured his sperm, sluggish, vanquished, winded, after only getting half an inch up the long canal to the place where Francey's eggs leaned out from the balcony of her uterus, calling out directions to no avail. Still, they were fast enough for the short walk from the syringe to the petri dish. The last hurdle to insemination.

Back in the sixties they used condoms, diaphragms, birth control pills, douches, everything they could think of *not* to get pregnant. They celebrated Francey's periods. But in the second year of a brand-new century they shuddered at the slightest pink stain— she'd switched from black to white underwear to keep track. They'd done the hormone shots. He'd taken herbs. They'd both stopped drinking. She'd seen a shaman. They'd both been to counseling. Nothing worked.

At midlife, nothing was turning out like he thought. Not marriage, with all its hope and misgivings, and certainly not fatherhood, how impossible it had proven to be to impregnate the woman he loved. They'd decided to cut their losses. Sell the house, pay off the mortgage, hit the road. Setting out on an adventure to reclaim their wanderlust that had been on the back burner for the last three years, all their resources that had been focused on fertilization finally freed up for travel, they'd wound up in a bone yard of the desert, the creator's workshop. No verdant oasis, at least not yet, anyway. Fruitfulness and multiplication just didn't seem to be in their cards. Maybe adventure would be. They weren't too old for that.

And now here they are in Terlingua, whatever that really means. It seems important to know—a riddle, a koan. There's something he needs to understand, something about empathy, get out of his own grief and cross the bridge back to her. That's what the counselor said. His life may depend on it. Hers, too. But the new surroundings so far have only accentuated the desolation he feels. Francey had said it looked wonderful. How could they be on such opposite sides?

He looks around in this cavernous bar in the desert, at the couple in the bar placing their tuned instruments on a rack the size of a medium-sized tree. The woman with the shot-up guitar gets up behind the microphone first.

"Ten minutes, Tanya," Mike the bartender says to her. "I mean it this time."

Tanya starts singing after a long instrumental comprised of two alternating minor chords. Rooney counts. He played the bass in the school band in junior high. Eventually she starts to sing. She stops. "I forgot to say this is an original song," she says. Then she starts all over again. Thirty-two verses later the husband has run off with the sister of the woman who threw herself off a bridge. A lot happened in between that he can't quite remember. Bobby Gentry meets Ralph Stanley in this very song, in this very bar. It's enough to make your head spin.

Rooney applauds and whistles. He's glad the song is over but he likes the way she bows humbly, grateful for the chance to sing. And isn't that what open mics are? Open? Isn't that still worth fighting for—one small freedom? A single voice crying in the white noise of the wilderness?

But Tanya must have thought she'd turned the mic off when she says "Snowbird," with great disdain. Everyone hears it.

"Oops," she says. "Sorry."

No wonder her boyfriend shot her guitar, and the telescope, too. He'd seen enough. Rooney knows he's probably not above that kind of psychotic comeback. "I am not a snowbird," he says slowly, enunciating every syllable like the middleclass white guy he is. "I'm from Texas. I did not come down here from Iowa with Triple-A triptychs and an itinerary. I'm winging it, just like you," he says, surprised at himself for saying it, because it's starting to be true. Again. A fledgling claim upon the vast territory of entropy.

She nods. "I can see that now," she says. And what does she see—some glimmer of the pole vaulter in his eye? Some old hand stamp still glowing in the dark from his very first Doors concert in Dallas? Or only a tinge of anti-anxiety meds tamping the flow of adrenalin?

He raises his now-empty shot glass at her. Mike the bartender leans forward with the bottle to refill it—on the house—but Rooney puts his hand over the top the way you do in communion when you want the priest to think you're still on the wagon. He knows when to stop. Right now. Time to quit while he's ahead. Alcohol and Xanax definitely don't mix. It says so right on the orange bottle with the child-proof cap. Tomorrow he'll stop taking it. There's nothing left to be anxious about. It's over. He wants his energy and passion back, his ability to get truly worked up about something. But right now he can't get off the stool quite yet and has to sit there for a while until he can get his balance back. It's not about alcohol; it's about finding his center of gravity again. Maybe it's not a meltdown coming, just a run of the mill midlife tailspin.

The couple from the Love Bug go up next. "Play 'All Along the Watchtower,'" Tanya calls out. But the woman says to her, "We don't know a thing you would want to hear." She doesn't say it mean, mostly just feisty. The bartender laughs. Tanya blushes. There's an awful moment where somebody could get shot here. But then Tanya laughs, lifts a glass to the couple. "Your pleasure, then," she says.

And they please themselves. And everyone listening. They launch into some bluegrassy tune, "Lost Little Children," of all things, which somehow suits this bomb shelter at the edge of a ghost town in the Chihuahua desert. The man plays one of two banjoes. When they finish with the song he says to his partner, "One of us is out. You're sharp." She glares at him, whips out an apparatus with a roach clip on the end that she clips to a tuning peg. "It's never you," she says. "Why don't you blame the banjo for a change?"

Maybe all is not lovely in the Love Bug, after all. She satisfies herself with checking the tuning, unclips the tuner, and tosses it to him. "You're flat," she says. And laughs. There's a long pause during which all hell could break loose. Minds snapped and wars were fought over less. Then, somehow, he laughs with her. All is well, or could be, soon. He tunes the flat string and they play another song. They're not bad. In fact, pretty good. And they actually move and show some heart up there, not like the family bands Rooney's seen up in Waco or over in Tres Rios that stand straight as sticks and barely move their mouths. They're more likely from the folkie crowd at Kerrville.

Francey should be here, he thinks. He really wants to share this with her. But she's probably up there practicing her Spanish with the tamale lady, learning another language he won't be able to understand, finding beauty in a place that frightens him. She's probably not even aware that he's gone, that in a very real sense, a necessary sense, some part of him is ready to disappear.

The lights waver. Something big crashes above. Rooney fully

expects the ceiling to creak and groan, like a rickety mine shaft while white, ominous dust sifts down from splintering rafters. There's another crash. Incoming? But no, it's only thunder. The couple pauses mid-song, but go on playing. The microphone's dead but they just sing louder to compensate. The lights go out all together but they never stop singing—they're good pickers if they don't have to look at what their fingers are doing. And their harmonies stay close together. If they keep singing everything will be all right.

"Devil's back in Presidio, I guess," Mike the bartender says to Tanya as he strikes a match and lights a Virgin of Guadalupe candle on the bar.

"Yeah," she says, "throwing those brass balls around Ojinaga. Maybe he should aim for Lajitas this time. Tyson's in town."

Rooney doesn't know what she's talking about, but Mike does.

"I think they were supposed to be bronze, those balls," he says. "And I hope he aims for Crawford next time."

Rooney tries again to get off the stool.

"Better stay put," Mike says. "Sounds like the real deal. The creek will probably flash."

The rain pounds the roof like a truckload of ball bearings dumped from a great height all at once. The Jamboree—will she hold? Did he remember to set the parking brake? Pity Sake must be having conniptions by now. And Francey? She's probably holding on to the door frame of the motor home like the crew of the wreck of the Hesperus watching west Texas wash away.

This is *weather*, he thinks. A lot of it.

Francey steps out of the Jamboree into a rising puddle. She's cupping her hands around her mouth calling through the wind for the cat. There aren't any cottonwood trees for it to run up. But it has made its frantic feline way up one of the sawed-off, six-foot trunks. It clings to the top yowling, ears flat. Francey climbs onto the picnic table, stepping over the splintered end. The wind whips her hair, her shirt flaps like a sail. She stretches out her arms. She thinks it might just be possible to fly, not very far. Thirty feet in Kitty Hawk was enough to change history. *Fly*.

She doesn't feel frightened or in danger. In the midst of this storm a strange calm comes over her. The worst has already happened as far as she's concerned. She's glad to be anywhere but the home they left. Inside that house, in its pine-paneled nooks and crannies, something lurked. She used to look at Rooney and think it was his fault. It had to be his fault. She had plenty of eggs. Or at least enough. He was looking at her the same way, probably. The tests were inconclusive in terms of who had the right components; "in theory," the first fertility doctor said, "you should be able to conceive." Conceive. As if the concept had to take hold in the mind before the body understood what was wanted. They'd stumbled their way to the last hurdle, the *in vitro* milepost. At nine thousand dollars the stakes were staggeringly high. They knew they couldn't afford to do it more than once; everything was riding on this egg, this little long shot. She'd worried about it, silently dividing in the dish, naked in the lab under a lamp late at night. She'd seen a film, she knew how the sperm was poured into a syringe, how the egg resisted the needle, became concave at its insistent point. Then, with a little push, the needle was in and the egg relaxed, became egg-shaped again after the needle was withdrawn. But fertilization looked painful in the video. She wondered if it was. If the egg, thus fertilized, rebelled. She doesn't blame it. She applauds her egg's rebel heart. It knew better. It had wanted to swim in a bath of sperm, to be penetrated by tiny, round tadpole, not a needle of surgical steel pushed by a latex-covered hand.

All of that seems far away from Terlingua. The wind and the coming storm blow it free as she turns, the winding sheet of shame coming loose, shredding itself in air. Where is Rooney? The thought comes to her then dissipates. He's where he is. She's right here. On a picnic table in a cockeyed campground. "Pity Sake!" she cries and suddenly realizes that anyone listening would have no idea she was calling a cat. They'd think she was one of those shouters, people turned out of mental institutions, shouting out everything they thought but had never said out loud.

The cat yowls. Then it jumps, runs through the rain and thunder, a white streak with a tail. The black dog with the beads races after.

Rooney's off the stool now. The bartender bitches that he can't find another candle; the one he'd lit flutters threateningly. The Virgin isn't intervening in this one. Even candles are out of order here. Rooney stumbles across the floor. Is it his imagination, or is it raining on his head?

"Goddamn toilet," Mike yells. But the water's not coming from the john or the roof, it's running down the stairs through the open hatch. Rooney looks up through the rain, listens through the thunder and roar and high lonesome harmonies for Francey's voice calling out his name.

The cat flies through the open hatch, hissing, the dog with the Mardi Gras beads hot on its tail, and lands, claws out, right on Rooney's shoulder. He grabs it, tears it off his shoulder, and makes his way up the stairs against the water. By the time he gets to the Jamboree his hands are scratched all to hell, his T-shirt in tatters. His feet are soaked.

Francey's on the picnic table looking in the opposite direction, her arms out, her shirt flapping, slowly turning like a vane.

The rain stops abruptly and the river of water that just a minute ago was flowing through the so-called campground quickly soaks into the dirt. Camp Lake-When-it Rains is already drying up, leaving a gluey, viscous mud behind.

Francey turns toward him. The cat is nearly calm now under Rooney's arm as if he's found the only safe place in all of Texas and means to stay there. But Rooney's heart pounds as he hands Pity Sake up to Francey. He's winded from running with a traumatized cat whose paws never touched anything but carpet, across a muddy parking lot in a storm. No pole to place in that sweet spot and launch himself over the bar. The only bar he'd cleared was La Kiva, just barely. He's out of breath. He's scared. She could have been struck by lightning up there. She could be dead. He could be completely losing it by now.

"Did you get the envelope?" she asks.

"Did I *what?*"

"The envelope—to pay."

What a woman. What a memory. The only envelope around is the one he's trying to push. So far, nothing's giving way.

She looks at him while she strokes the cat. He imagines himself, stroked like that. Would he feel soothed? Aroused? Grateful?

"It's free, Francey. All of it. As far as I can tell."

The storm moves on leaving only the tang of creosote in the air, dirt stained darker by rain, a lot of mud splattered on the Jamboree. The Love Bug couple comes back with all their instruments, deliberately splashing through the one remaining puddle. The dog with the pink necklace paws at the Love Bug. They let the dog in then put away the instruments, then get in their little green pickup and drive over to the picnic table. "Wanna go with us to the Starlight for dinner?" the man says.

Rooney and Francey look at each other, a silent signal passing between them. "Sure," they say, almost together, feeling like the new kids at school standing awkwardly in the cafeteria with their lunch trays until unexpectedly someone nice says, "Sit with us!" The tamales will keep.

Rooney stows Pity Sake in the Jamboree, tossing a catnip mouse into the cupboard, and they climb into the extracab of the couple's Toyota after they'd relocated a pile of books, CDs, newspapers, dog bowls, several moving violations, and two sacks of laundry into the back.

A white clay skeleton with a yellow clay guitar dangles from the rearview mirror. It has springs for legs and arms and bulbous clay appendages that serve as hands and feet. The hands look like boxing gloves as the figurine swings crazily from the motion of the truck lurching through potholes. Its feet kick wildly and his little white skull face smiles, beaming. He is so very happy to be hanging there dancing to the music on the radio instead of still stuck in the wigwam knickknack store where he'd probably spent his whole life waiting to be chosen.

"That's Felipe," the man says, noticing Rooney hypnotized in the rearview mirror. "Annie got him in San Antonio." He still hasn't introduced himself, but his name will come up, sooner or later.

Annie twists her long curly hair into a tail and clips it up, stray strands coming loose immediately.

"Where in Arkansas are you from?" Francey calls out.

"We're from here now," Annie calls back over her shoulder.

"You picked the best place to camp," the man driving says. "*De-*camp," he adds, "at La Kiva."

Rooney notes that he calls the place La Kiva, not Big Bend Travel Park like it says on the sign. He didn't pick this place. But it seems now that it's chosen him.

"No leash laws," Annie says appreciatively. "No buckle of the Bible belt. What a relief. But I'll always love Fayetteville."

"No envelopes," Rooney says. "It's a good thing."

Felipe's dancing to klezmer music, the kind that used to accompany Heckle and Jeckle cartoons. Annie gives Felipe a flick with her finger; the road is smooth enough so that's he's swinging more slowly now. He kicks it up again as they hit a pothole and the radio segues into the theme from Bonanza. "He's Tim's alter ego," she says, looking slyly at Tim.

So it's Tim. Not Timmy, thank God. All their names would rhyme. Rooney can't help but wonder about his own alter ego.

Does he have one? Maybe it's a little skeleton clinging to a pole, grinning helplessly, swinging frantically from the Jamboree's rearview mirror as Francey flicks him with her fingers. And the accompanying music? Bolero. Fanfare for the Common Man. Camp Granada.

They pass a wooden sign hung high between two posts. Terlingua.

Rooney thinks about the three languages the Canadian mentioned. English, Spanish, Comanche. Yes. No. Maybe. He hunches down to see through the oblong porthole of the tiny side window. There's a cemetery with weathered wooden crosses jumbled like pick-up sticks barely visible in the dusk. Miners, mostly, who came for the quicksilver, Tim is saying, that was used during the war for detonator caps on bombs. Some of them probably died from mercury poisoning. On the hillsides adobe ruins of the miners' houses melt back into the mud they came from and further up the hill, several have been resurrected with wood and rocks and tin. A school bus sinks to its rims in mud and looks as if it's been used for target practice. A smaller version of the Statue of Liberty stands forlornly in front of a rock shop hoisting her lighted torch toward Mexico.

So this is Terlingua, he thinks, getting an inkling now of what the Canadians alluded to. Where things happen you shouldn't necessarily try to explain. To ask means you just don't get it. He'll try not to ask from here on in. To roll with it, wherever it goes, even if it kills him.

The Starlight, when they pull up in front, looks surprisingly intact, its name beautifully painted in 1940-ish-style letters across the mission-style front. On the long porch connecting it to what looks like some kind of store a few characters like the ghosts of the miners themselves sit on a bench nursing their beers. A dogfight brews at the far end of the porch and a kid on a bicycle careens up and down the walkway. A man who's a dead ringer for Doc Holiday plays a mandolin. Beautifully. Tim and Annie go over to listen and agree to meet him the following afternoon to jam.

"I knew we should have brought the instruments," Tim says.

Quick on the draw, this couple, ready to play at the drop of a hat. Total hams. Rooney is starting to like them, hopes they're doing more than humoring him. Now the four of them push through the heavy wooden doors of the Starlight. It's like being part of an entourage. A lot of the people at the tables recognize Tim and Annie, not by name, exactly, but smile as they pass. Rooney sees the Canadian Club taking up every stool at the bar. They actually wave. Even Tanya, the woman with the shot-up guitar, is here, raises her glass to him.

"We played on the porch last week," Annie says. "The owner heard us and wants to book us for a gig next month. We'll hang out until then. Start looking for land to buy. Build a pole barn over the Love Bug. Collect rain water, go solar, the whole nine yards."

Tim looks at her, incredulous, as if he's learned something entirely new about her. Then he nods slowly in agreement.

Rooney wishes he hadn't given up playing the bass. That he hadn't given up on a lot of things. He could be jamming with them and Doc Holiday tomorrow. Francey could play the flute—or did they sell it in the yard sale? Together they could break on through to the other side. People would welcome them when they come into the Starlight. And he could say, "That's Terlingua for you," with irony and experience and even benevolence to the next greenhorns that roll into La Kiva without a hair dryer. How did Tim and Annie fit into this place so fast? The same way they fit into the Love Bug, probably, without a lot of fuss. Willingly.

The Starlight fills. The whole town must be here eating and drinking. There's one empty table in what looks like the former orchestra pit and above that a stage with a backdrop painted with cowboys and burros, cactus and campfires. In the sky above them, a silver swath of stars crowds the western sky.

"You just missed the Vagina Monologues last week," Annie says to Francey.

"Here?" she says. "No way!" She must know what Annie's talking about.

The Vagina Monologues? In the Starlight Theater in Terlingua? He doesn't dare ask. He tries to picture vaginas talking, the lips forming sultry, secret words. What would Francey's say? What *wouldn't* it say?

"So," Tim says to Rooney, "what brings you to this neck of the woods?"

Rooney thinks hard for a minute. Really hard. Nothing is coming to him. "We sold the house," he finally said.

"Just like that," Francey says, clapping her hands together once for punctuation. "We paid it off, too. We've been talking about traveling for the past ten years. Now we're really doing it. Not just for two weeks. For real."

"Good for you," Annie says. "They're like albatrosses—houses. Lifestyles. Maintenance nightmares."

But it was *our* albatross, Rooney thinks, almost nostalgic now for the place, its pine paneling and breakfast nook. "We might have been happy there . . ." he says out loud.

"But we weren't," Francey says. "It was killing us. Remember?"

She's wrong. It wasn't the house, it was what wasn't *in* the house. The sound of a child growing up in it. They should have had a child. A child to wish upon like a star with all its shine and mystery.

Now, he could end up on a patch of sand with a single cactus in it. Watch the stickers grow. It might be enough. It would have to be enough.

No aceptámos tarjetas de crédito. It's free. All of it. He'd waited too long. For a lot of things. To start a family, for one. To Get Real, whatever that was. And now here he is out on the road, without a good reason to give to this man here who asked him a simple question: What brings him to this neck of the woods? He's not certain of anything anymore. He'd gone to a palm reader just before he left. The sign on the highway by the mobile home park in the south side of Paris had said, "Predictions of the Future and the Past." Madame Zoza in a turban and kimono looked at his palm and said two things. "There was a fall. There will be a messenger." She was right about the fall. There had been more than one. So she could predict the past. But it's the messenger he's worried about. A messenger who will ask him a question that his life will, in some way, depend on his answering.

Tim is saying there didn't used to be a roof over this place. That's why they named it the Starlight. Once upon a time there was music here open to the stars and the acoustics were amazing. Tim goes on and on about it. Jerry Jeff Walker. Butch Hancock. "The ghost of Pancho Villa is right here, man," Tim says emphatically. "Him and Townes van Zandt. Maybe even Billy the Kid." Then somehow he's jumped the track entirely and is talking about Orphan Trains, about an "army of children given away in train stations across the country. Annie and I do a program about it in libraries," he says.

Rooney's never heard of such a thing; it's not something he ever learned in school and he really paid attention to history. Surely these people are fabricating. They look capable of concocting elaborate fictions. But no, they're not making it up. They've been to reunions of the survivors, they've been inspired, by this man here in a Polaroid in his eighties with his arms around both of them that's being passed around the table. Tim and Annie look like *his* children. They don't need children of their own. They've become their own children.

Rooney looks up at the solid roof and can't even imagine looking up at the stars shining down on him. He can't imagine orphans standing on platforms in train stations or on stages at opera houses, like this theater, here. Rooney looks up at the stage, at the place where they could have stood waiting, stunned by the emptiness of the country they'd crossed after the crowded places they'd come from. He would choose one in a heartbeat if he had the chance. But he only sees himself up there, small, alone. Unchosen.

He gets up from the table to find the restroom.

"It's outside," Tim says. "In what used to be the old jail."

When Rooney finds it there's a line waiting and it didn't come from the Starlight alone. It must serve the entire Ghost Town. But he doesn't want to pee in jail.

He wanders across the parking lot looking for a place to piss on his own, freely. He steps into desert scrub, carefully avoiding the prickly pear. He stops short in front of one of the adobe walls. It's not much of a barrier; he keeps going, up its undulating edge, arms out for balance. He used to have perfect balance; now he teeters. He stops where it meets another wall, plants a foot on either side of the corner. He unzips. Breathes, lets go, pissing into the ruin of an adobe, some miner's home sweet home that's been dissolving for years into the ground it was made from. Somewhere in the distance, he hears drumming. He looks up at the stars. They swarm above his head, silver bees in a mercury stream that goes on and on without end, undulating toward the moon. It's almost more than he can bear, the infinity. It's so visible here. How little he knows. How much he wants to understand.

From where he stands, shaking off, he can hear Francey's delighted laughter all the way from the Starlight. At him? Is it his fault? Did the doctor tell her something she kept secret? He'd rather not know. It's never far away, the doubt. It's followed him, even here, and the hard part is, lately that doubt seems to be leaving Francey be.

He looks down at his penis dangling from his open fly. At least it isn't small. One last golden drop refuses to fall, a low motility universe swimming within. He yanks the zipper closed.

The kid he saw earlier on the bicycle pedals by. "Hey," he says to Rooney and stops.

"Hey," Rooney answers, grateful he's not invisible, that this Terlinguan child is not laughing at him. He looks Mexican. Or American. Or maybe Comanche. Or all of the above. Does he speak one language, or all three? Maybe he's the messenger Madame Zoza predicted.

"What're you doing up there?" the kid asks, not challenging, just curious, one leg out to balance the bike.

Rooney's mind seizes up, as if he's been called on in class and is completely unprepared. *The question.*

After a minute the kid says again, "Hey, mister. What're you doing?"

"Trying not to fall," Rooney says.

There is no going back. There's only this unknowable space in front of him he tries to sense with his hands. All he knows for certain is that he feels inexplicable gratitude for this kid. Because he saw a man balanced on a wall in the dark and cared enough to ask, because he had an answer. But was this the question or would there be others? This one was too easy.

He remembers Tanya in the bar talking about Burro Judy disappearing into Mexico. It could happen to him. He could walk and keep on walking, like Harry Dean Stanton in the movie *Paris, Texas,* only in reverse. There wouldn't be any envelopes to find. No instrument begging to be played. No child waiting to be conceived. No woman to frustrate and hold her hope hostage. Just walking. Into Mexico, where the line between here and there blurs by what's left of a great river you could leap across if you got a running start, or so he'd heard. A different statue of liberty would hold a torch to welcome him to the land of the brave he's never been but can still become.

"Awesome," the kid says, as if he's heard all of Rooney's thoughts. But the only thing Rooney actually said out loud was that he was trying not to fall. Which is true, the only thing he can claim right here and now.

The kid rides on, the bicycle wavering, once, as he gets up to speed.

And it is awesome, the fact that he's here. Still here. But it's Francey, Francey holding a flashlight now, turning it on him. Will she recognize the effort, this man not falling off a wall, this middle-aged orphan ready to take a leap even if he is only four or five feet off the ground?

"There you are," she says, as if she's just discovered him.

He doesn't turn around. He stands there looking out at the almost full moon clearing the Chisos. A partly deflated thing, still rising like a sad balloon, southeast out of Mexico.

He tries to remember the word for moon, the woman's lonely face, "*La luna,*" he says, tentatively.

"*És verdad,*" Francey says.

"What did you say?" he says, turning, almost losing his balance.

"I said, 'it's the truth.' At least, that's what I think I said." She holds out her arm for him to grab if he needs it. He doesn't.

"*És verdad,*" he repeats. But he's not sure, not sure of anything. Here, even the truth could be mistaken for something else.

Francey sings off key in the shower. She soaps her breasts, her thighs, works up a slippery lather between her legs. The water pressure is barely a trickle, but she doesn't mind. She rinses her body slowly, watching the suds go down the drain.

She dries off, pours herself a cup of coffee. The electricity's working just fine. She sits down on the plaid couch with the towel wrapped around her. She props her feet up on the walnut veneer coffee table and studies her toes. Annie had told her she has some gold nail polish, and today Francey's ready to be more frivolous; she's put in a lot of overtime being on standby. Why not adorn herself, even lavishly, start wearing a lot of heavy silver jewelry, something to keep her grounded. Her body had been through the wringer in the last three years, mega hormones stripped her down to fighting weight. If she wasn't careful, a good gust of wind might blow her away.

Rooney ventured out on the Vespa at sunrise. Good for him. So far, this trip is doing him wonders. What was it his counselor said? "Your husband will be like a man landing on the moon, worried about what that first step will look like, taking his time to step out. But he's the kind of guy who'll take the leap, sooner or later. Just give him a lot of room; he'll surprise you."

She did. He does. Just when you think you've got him pegged as lazy, he does something that requires extraordinary, meticulous effort, like cleaning and polishing every single inch of the piano before he gave it away. Just when you think he's self-centered he stays up all night holding your hand when you're worried sick. Just when you think he's unforgiving of himself he learns to take a compliment without shoving it away. And just when you think he's going to keep soaring a while, he falters, falls flat on his ass. There isn't any pattern to Rooney. No rhyme or reason. She'd given up predicting what he'd do in any given situation. Still, there are times when she has her heart in her mouth and it has nothing to do with him. It's the "Now What?" feeling, the question she has no answer for, for herself. She's not going to be a mother. Adoption is out of the question; they'd both agreed on that. Too risky—fetal alcohol syndrome only the tip of the iceberg. She knew it was selfish, but they'd wanted a child they'd made themselves. No substitutions. "Now what," indeed.

Somehow, it's his drama—the whole thing, not hers. And maybe that's her fate—taking care of the child *in* him rather than from him. He was an only child of a stern career military father and a pharmaceutically sedated mother. She, however, had four good-natured, hefty brothers, parents who at least seemed to get along, at least in the living room. So, for Rooney, having a family had higher stakes. She's beginning to see, in hindsight, in the long sightlines the desert provides, that having a child might have been Rooney's desperate attempt to finally have somebody to play with.

This trip was his idea, mostly. Where is he headed? Maybe he'll know when he gets there. Left to her own devices, she'd find a room with a view somewhere, probably Wyoming or Montana. Look out the window at a vast, gorgeous emptiness. Write. About what? Fiction or nonfiction? The first line has yet to come to her, like a search party still weaving back and forth below the endless horizon line.

Through the window she can see Annie and Tim sitting in

their chairs beneath the Love Bug's awning. Their dog rolls in the dirt happily, scratching her back, stirring up the dust. Pity Sake watches with curious disdain, this thing that could eat him. The cottonwood stump has become his pedestal now that he's regained a little of his lost dignity from last night, washing his paws to prove it. He no longer wants inside.

"Hey," she calls out the window to Tim and Annie. "Be right out."

She pulls on her jeans and a T-shirt, slides into sandals. Sandals! In February! Out the door to join the neighbors on this first morning in Terlingua.

And it's a fine morning, rain washed and clear. The Canadian Club is just coming back from a predawn bicycle trip, sweaty and ready for Bloody Marys, their children old enough to be their friends, their guides. Comraderie, not dependency. The pot of gold at the end of the years of raising them.

Teresa, the tamale lady, makes a beeline for the Canadian compound with a plate piled high. She comes back a few minutes later with a twenty. She waves it at Francey as she walks by.

"*Tamales?*" Teresa says.

"*No, gracias. Mañana,*" Francey says. She still has the ones she bought last night.

"*Mañana,*" Teresa says back. "OK."

Tim and Annie load up the pickup with water jugs, snacks for their excursion to the hot springs.

"Ready to go to paradise?" Annie calls out.

"Not until you paint my toenails gold," Francey says.

"Oh yeah, I almost forgot," Annie says and disappears inside the Love Bug. Francey sticks her head in the door. She's surprised; it's bigger than it looks. From the outside what looks like a toaster feels as cozy as a sailboat cabin, everything rounded, rumpled, lived in.

Annie finds the nail polish in a drawer full of duct tape, guitar strings, henna, and ibruprofen, and, Francey can't help but notice, condoms, and says, "I can't believe it was the first place I looked."

Outside in the chairs beneath the awning, Annie tells Francey to put her feet in her lap.

Delighted, Francey leans back in the lawn chair, her feet in Annie's lap and closes her eyes, feeling the application of the glittering polish with the tiny brush, like eyelashes fluttering against her toenails leaving liquid gold behind.

"I thought I heard Rooney take off," Annie says. "When's he coming back?"

"Oh, he left early, took the long way down. He'll meet us there."

"Fearless," Annie says.

"Yeah, he can be. Wonder what they call us?"

"High-flying bitches, probably."

"Sometimes they'd be right. I've secretly wanted to be one."

"I've been practicing," Annie says.

Francey doesn't say any more. She doesn't know Annie well enough, and besides, she doesn't need to get into the whole lick log here. If she starts, she might not be able to stop. She's on vacation from all of that. Beginning right now.

Annie blows on Francey's toes to dry the polish. Her breath feels warm, wonderful. Her toes are jewels now, worthy of Cleopatra. She's sorry to have to put on socks and shoes.

Tim ties up the dog on a long red leash, sets out a blue bowl of water. He starts up the truck and Francey climbs in back with the provisions. Teresa's tamales. Water. Sunscreen. Hats. Annie says they can put the Vespa in the back for the ride home when they hook up with Rooney.

They drive out of La Kiva, Felipe swinging from the mirror to KYOT Radio. Mitch Miller, Joe Ely, Rickie Lee Jones. *Thus Spoke Zarathustra*, forever associated with the theme from 2001 and that strange monolith found on the moon. They could have filmed it here. Past the music store and coffee shop, the river tour headquarters. Francey can see it all now that she's not having to search

for a campground or to have her antennae up for Rooney's shifting moods. She could live here. She already is. Why go any farther?

They come upon a flea market by the Hungry Javelina restaurant. Beneath an awning, karaoke. A woman sings Dolly Parton,
or tries to.

Tim slows down, eyeing the wares. Tools, clothes, paperback
novels. Puppies.

"I want two," Tim says.

"Don't even think about it," Annie says.

But Francey does. She just might come back later for one. Give
Pity Sake something real to yowl about. She herself might sing like
Dolly Parton. It could happen.

They pass up the puppies and the karaoke, what passes for day-
time activity here, and head through Study Butte for the national
park, slowing down slightly at the kiosk so the ranger can see their
week pass taped to the windshield. She waves them through.

They climb steadily toward the Chisos, past the turnoff to Old
Maverick Road, sticking to the main road through Panther
Junction, then turn south toward Rio Grande Village.

"We tried to go there," Francey says. "It was full."

"Good thing," Tim says. "It's like a big parking lot for RVs.
Full of snowbirds with satellite dishes. They all go to bed at seven
thirty. It was fate that brought you to La Kiva."

Fate. Yes. Well. She'd had her fill of her fate. Fate was no fun.
This is happenstance. Nothing ordained, just stumbled upon. Safer
for being so.

The Vespa kicks up a respectable trail of dust as Rooney heads
down Old Maverick Road, all twenty horsepower stretching out.
The kiosk at the park entrance was closed, but he took a map from
a pile left on the counter.

Rooney can't get past 10 mph, not because of the horsepower
limitations, but because Old Maverick Road has the surface of cor-

rugated tin. His whole body vibrates from the rough terrain beneath the two little wheels designed for urban streets.

He's glad he made the decision to head out on his own, to meet up with everyone later. It's a part of the new life, the change he's making. He remembers a theater exercise he'd done in college for a drama class. The technique was called "Do It Wrong" and it entailed becoming conscious of all the automatic things one did and making a point of doing it differently—to get at the true essence of things—walking backward through the house, picking up the phone with his feet. Now he's tooling down Old Maverick Road. The name appeals to him. It's how he feels: like a lone dogie cut out of the herd happily exploring, even if the stupid Vespa is shaking out his teeth. He wishes he had a horse instead.

The temperature's a seductive sixty-five already, not a cloud in the sky. What had seemed like nothing but rocks yesterday in the Jamboree begin to look interesting. The Creator's leftovers. He'd already made what He'd planned; here, He didn't have to try so hard. Rooney lets his eyes wander from one side of the road to the other, weaves the Vespa back and forth. He hasn't felt this good in years.

The insides of the very earth he's been living on have broken through the crust of the world here, exposing itself at last to him now that he looks. The rocks rise from the desert floor, a muscular arrangement of all the colors in the paint box he'd avoided: the deeper colors, subtler hues. Some formations curve, rounded like a breast. Others jumble together like petrified logs. Or point like mule ears into a humbling expanse of sky.

Gray stalks splay in all directions like a bouquet of whips. When he looks more closely, he can see they actually have produced orange tips as bright as flames on candles. He stops, actually stops to look more closely. He checks the brochure he picked up at the kiosk at the park entrance. *Ocotillo.* If Francey were here she would reach right out to touch this fleshy bloom. The way she'd once held his penis in both hands, bringing him in. He can't even remember how that felt, making love for the sheer pleasure of it, not the desperate task of procreation; it seems so long ago. The orange buds, hard as cranberries, cluster at the end of the spiny sticks. In another few weeks they'll open to ruby-throated hummingbirds.

Next to the ocotillo, prickly pear, flat as beaver's tails studded with spikes. Punk plants with piercings. In another month they'll have something to show, too. Will he be here to see it? He could choose a cactus, sit by it, and wait. A steward of the desert. More than enough to do for a lifetime.

The scenic route is taking longer than he thought. A vehicle races up behind him and blows by, honking, leaving him in a cloud. The Canadian Club. He can see the Suburban's progress for miles afterward, a speeding silver bullet plowing the long, brown valley, a skein of dust hanging in the air behind it.

He tastes the dust, feels it in every pore as he continues southward. He stops to let it settle. He turns his attention to a pair of ravens, their voices like epithets as they come in for a landing on an outcropping nearby. They disappear inside. He'd always thought of ravens as solitary birds, dreary hermits, oracles of doom like his father reading the stock reports, but there are two of them here, probably working on expanding their vocabulary from the one word Edgar Allen Poe had assigned to them, changing it ever so slightly. Evermore is a totally different thing.

The dust clears. The ravens take their time doing whatever it is ravens do when they're out of sight. The Vespa spurts gravel on takeoff and settles into a blender-like whine. Rooney holds his feet out to either side in a V when he goes downhill like he did when he was trying to master his first bicycle while his father angrily shouted instructions from the driveway. He tried not to wobble, then or now.

He comes upon a sign that says "Luna's Jacal." He stops, not having a clue what a *jacal* is. Or where to look for it. Luna seems to apply to the landscape rather than something in the sky. He puts the Vespa on its kickstand and walks past the sign. And there it is, a miniature version of La Kiva. A cairn of rocks and a roof made of sticks. He reads the sign, about the Luna family that once lived in this dwelling, the *jacal* (pronounced ha-kahl, the sign tells him) is not much bigger than a good-sized grave. He bends down to look through the opening that serves as a window. It's dark inside. A bare floor, a little light coming through a few chinks. He expects to see a pile of charred bones in the corner. He tries to imagine himself living inside such a thing. He'd always thought that prairie sod houses must have been creepy; this thing is a tomb.

How did the Luna family live in a hole in the ground in the desert? He looks around. Someone has vandalized what the park rangers put up as a barricade. In spite of his aversion to cramped spaces, he crawls inside. It's no bigger than a playhouse.

He sits there, cross-legged, a sentient being inside a rock hut listening to what the wind has to say, its entire repertoire from whisper to moan to howl and back again. An animal burrows next door.

What did the Luna family have in this *jacal?* A cooking pot, a blanket, a burro hobbled outside. What did the children play with? What did the father do to provide for them?

There's nothing. No one. Not even wind now or the ghosts of the Luna family. Just the desert sanding itself down a second at a time. He leaves the *jacal* behind.

The road is endless, full of twists and hairpin turns, desolate country populated only by abandoned mines and shattered homesteads. He heads further south, keeping what's left of the setting sun on his right. He finds the river road and follows it, east now. It's so close, that other country. He feels its pull, how it wants him to cross over, how easily he could.

He stops to examine one of the ruins. Bigger than the *jacal,* but roofless, like the Starlight had once been. The scavenger in him can't help but poke through a pile of rusty cans in a corner. Relics from the days of tin. He stops. He thinks he hears something.

He listens. There is a sound now, besides the wind. It's the Vespa, starting up. He runs out the door just in time to see a man taking off, heading south, toward Mexico. He runs after it but he's soon swallowed in the trail of dust left behind.

Francey presses her face to the window as Tim takes a turnoff to the hot springs, a dirt road winding downhill. They pass several primitive campgrounds. Not much different from La Kiva if you couldn't find a gray box that worked. In one spot, a man sits in a metal folding chair by a van, roasting some meat on a stick. Further down the road, a couple in a small RV have a generator going.

The road ends in a dirt parking lot next to an adobe ruin. They carry the water and the snacks past the remains, a sign says, of what was once a post office and general store, the remnants of a motel from the forties, all of it sun bleached and vacant but devoid of trash and graffiti. They stop to look inside the little motel, the half dozen rooms hardly more than stone cells adorned with faded murals—men in sombreros, women in shawls, blanketed burros. Despite the art there's something almost medieval about it, a room where some penitent who'd just crossed the desert barefoot could kneel down and confess to incendiary lust before he let himself be led to water.

The path narrows and winds through a grove of salt cedar at least ten feet high clinging to the river and continues past an enormous palm tree; behind it, a lagoon, sultry with blue water gracefully slides through a sandstone sluice at the end of a long, languid pool.

Before long, they hear voices. Others are here before them— three people sitting waist deep in a shallow, roughly poured, small concrete pool. A skinny man with a floppy hat, Ray Bans, and shorts, a couple in bathing suits loll in the hot water, smiling as they shift positions to make room for the new arrivals.

Francey looks across the Rio Grande. She expected it to be bigger with such a name, but so much has been taken from it along the way. Cities, subdivisions, farms. It's shallow, maybe thirty feet across choked with salt cedar, that greedy foreign invader sucking up the water, or so the guidebook had said. In spite of everything, it flows. On the other side, Mexico looks a lot like Texas. Except for the people sitting in the sand by a fire. That's what they warm themselves with; there is no hot spring on their side. Boys, mostly, a few men. One man on a horse rides through the thicket of salt cedar, stops to speak to them for a minute, the horse shifting from one leg to the other, swishing his tail. The man nudges the horse with his bare heels and rides on.

Francey and Tim and Annie settle into the hot, soothing water. Introductions all around. The couple say they're from California and this is their second time in Big Bend. They're camping in a tent, they say, near Rooney's Place.

"That's my husband's name," Francey says. "What's this place like?"

"Ruins, not too far from Glen Springs," the man says.

"Oh," Francey says, disappointed.

"It's a great view," the woman adds.

The skinny man in the hat says he's from Wisconsin. "Been here since the annual chili cookoff," he says, "back in November. Don't seem to be able to leave just yet. Maybe I'll stay 'til the next one comes around."

"We heard about that cookoff," Tim says. "Always wanted to go to a world championship of something."

"A shitload of people come—over ten thousand last year from all over. You wouldn't believe how many Germans."

"Where do they put ten thousand people?" Francey asks. "Certainly not at La Kiva."

"La Kiva, the Boathouse, the parking lot at the store, the ranch up at CASI, the side of the road . . . and there's almost as many cops. DPS comes down here just to set up roadblocks and bust people. But they can't stop it. Lots of music. Lots of chili. You name it, it's all in happening in Terlingua." He lights up a joint, takes a hit, and passes it to the couple from California. They partake, then pass to Tim and Annie, who hold up their hands to decline.

Francey leans forward across the concrete pool to take it. Why not? Just to see if it's the way she remembered. The last time she smoked was at the Armadillo Headquarters in Austin. A lifetime ago.

She takes a deep drag on the joint, coughs, hands it back to the skinny man from Wisconsin. Her whole body floods with that sweet slowdown. She begins to admire the gold paint job on her toes. So does he. And his gaze feels as fluid and real as a brush stroke traveling up her legs, painting her pink as he goes.

The people across the river are coming toward them now, sticks in hand. Francey looks at them, moving in slow motion, in time with her slowed responses, slogging through the water. Is this a raid? A holdup? They don't look in an attacking mood. Their pants, wet to the knees from the crossing, make them look vulnerable, somehow.

"Are they illegals?" Francey asks. "They're certainly not trying to hide it."

"No," the man from Wisconsin says. "They live in Boquillas. They come across to sell things. Since Nine-Eleven you can't go over there. Oh, you can go but you can't get back in without a five-thousand-dollar fine or a year in jail or both. Unreal. When I was here three years ago you used to be able to walk over there or they'd get you in a boat if the water was up and take you back to a little place they'd set up with tables and lots of great food and beer. That's all gone now. Border Patrol watches from the bluffs. Our good neighbors to the south are screwed."

The people from Boquillas come ashore just downstream, then appear through the salt cedar curtain at the edge of the pool to show their carved walking sticks, their brightly painted stones, scorpions made of twisted copper wire and beads.

Nobody seems to have any money. Except the man from Wisconsin who looks closely at all their wares, ready to make a selection. Francey likes him, his ability to communicate with them in their language, his knowledge of the place. The way he looked at her with clear, uncluttered desire.

"*Mañana*," he says to the youngest, a boy of maybe fourteen.

Francey wonders why he didn't say so before, before they got wet crossing the river. What a jerk. He has the power to say "tomorrow," to make them go back across, to come back the next day and start over again. She submerges her feet, drowns those golden toes. She doesn't want him to look at them anymore. She wishes she had brought some money to give the boy.

Silently, the Mexicans turn and walk slowly back across the river. They return to Mexico with their sticks and stones and hunker down by the fire again, drying their wet shoes and pants, waiting for the next arrivals at the hot springs.

"Some of their stuff's not bad," the man from Wisconsin says. "The same sticks sell for fifteen up at Terlingua Trading Company."

No sooner has he finished saying this than a horde of prepubescent girls comes skittering down the path with several adult women trudging along behind. The girls throw their daypacks in a pile, strip down to their bathing suits, and jump into the water, squealing and splashing and shoving each other. "Eighth grade from Alpine," one of the adults, a hefty woman in khaki pants and a straw cowboy hat, says. "Field trip."

"Oh man," the woman from California says to her husband or boyfriend. "We're out of here. Being around a bunch of kids is not my idea of a vacation."

The man from Wisconsin leaves, too. Good riddance, Francey thinks. He's just a colonial dressed in Eddie Bauer gear, ogling those girls as he goes.

But Francey's enjoying watching these girls, their lithe, seamless bodies with only the beginnings of breasts, their legs still gleaming with tiny, golden hairs. Their self-consciousness is enormous. Singly, they would be shy, but as a group, this collective shyness quickly transforms into a high-pitched performance. They do and they don't want everybody to notice them. They glance across the river, prancing in the shallows, unsure of the attention they might get, not sure they want it from Mexico. One girl, a silky blond with a hot pink bikini and a spangley silver ankle bracelet, announces, "I have to pee! I'm going to wade into the middle of the river so I can pee in Mexico!" Her friends squeal at the very audacity of her, watch her slow progress toward the approximate center, the invisible line between their world and the one on the other side.

The girl squats down. Her face has a look of concentration for a second, then she starts laughing. "I'm peeing in Mexico!" she cries.

The teachers aren't paying any attention; they're looking for petroglyphs on the canyon wall.

Francey watches the girl, looks over the blond, shining head of hair to the boys on the other side. They're watching, too. Aside from universal teenage lust, what are they thinking as they watch this girl, so sure of herself and the boundaries that protect her that she can let loose a hot stream of urine right through that pink bikini?

Annie looks like she doesn't know whether to laugh or cry. Francey stares both stoned and transfixed by the tableau before her.

The girl in the river comes back to America, dripping, satisfied. The other girls step back, a little in awe, maybe even a little afraid of her. The eyes of the boys across the river follow her as she dries off with a brightly flowered towel from her backpack and plops herself down on a rock, putting on the headphones to her Walkman. Even from where Francey sits, she can hear the tinny sounds that escape the headphones, the rattling of a frenetic rhythm no one else can clearly hear but her.

Francey points at the girl. With the other index finger she makes three outward strokes. Shame. Shame. Shame on you. Not for her blatant sexuality, but for flaunting it in the face of an impoverished people, her relieving herself in the shared river a pink epithet flipped in a southerly direction.

The girl looks at her and turns the Walkman up higher.

Annie looks at Francey, throwing out a lifeline. Two women, one in middle age, the other still several exits away, both watching the next generation stake its considerable claim upon the future.

The teachers round the girls up. Soon enough, they're gone, back up the path to their bus or whatever they'd come in, taking their eighth-grade sass back to Alpine.

"Were we like that?" Annie says to Francey. "I mean, were we so arrogant we could announce we could piss on another country? And then actually do it?"

"No," Francey says. "Back then we were hiding beneath our desks waiting for a nuclear bomb. These days we have a president that pisses on other countries for us." But they both know the question Annie asked has another answer. No, we weren't like that. We aren't like that now. That girl is at the peak of her fecundity and doesn't even know it. Her ovaries are churning out thousands of eggs, unbeknownst to her. When the fertilized egg was implanted in Francey's womb she turned all her attention inward. She heard her own blood in her veins, felt the egg clinging to the wall of her uterus, imagined the heartbeat that would begin, imperceptibly at first, then louder like a drum. But for all that listening, she hadn't heard it let go, hadn't felt it falling through the crevice of the long canal. A silent passing. What should have been a cry was no more than a whisper, a pale pink stain on white cotton panties.

Across the river, the boys haven't moved. They stare, it seems to Francey, at the place where the girl in the pink bikini squatted down, where that hot stream laced with estrogen flows through the waters that pass their village, where, this very minute, their mothers could be washing their clothes in the same river, hanging them in the sun to dry.

The River Road winds endlessly, rutted worse than Old Maverick. Rooney puts one foot in front of the other. There has been no other vehicle. There will never be another vehicle. The Vespa? Good riddance, in the grand scheme of things. Maybe he's being tested. He hopes he's up to the task.

Nothing now but the sound of his feet, his heart, his body, moving alone through the wilderness like a tiny wooden boat upon an ocean without end.

And it was an ocean once. It still is. Places where the streams spilled down from the mountains in last night's rain cut deep gullies. The road's still muddy, slick in places, and Rooney has to pay attention to avoid slipping, his shoes literally stuck, especially in the stretches of road that form the beds of the washes, deep as a trench through the desert scrub.

He hasn't used his body like this since he was a teenager. It still works, but barely. For fifty-one, he's badly out of shape. His body had become, since he fell at age twenty, a body he could no longer believe in, a suit of skin that doesn't fit him any more.

Rooney had come close to being a pole-vaulting champion in college. That's what Francey really fell in love with. A short but well-built, well-read jock with long hair tied back who ran so fast with a pole three times his height and pitched himself gracefully and forcefully into thin air. He learned to find that sweet spot to place the pole in the box and rose, up and up, twisting at the exact moment he needed to, pushing back the pole and letting go, turning his thumbs inward so his elbows would clear the bar as his body arched, his feet already over the other side. He flew and in those few airborne seconds he sensed something in himself that he knew he might not be able to hold onto. For all that physical, momentary grace, he turned out not to be Olympic material. Not even close. He fell one day, coming over the bar badly. A concussion. Blurred vision. A broken pelvis. Chronic pain wasn't far behind. In a very real sense, he never came completely back. The best part of himself was still in midair. He took a job at Texas Instruments. He spent nineteen years behind a terminal, nineteen seasons at home mowing a lawn he'd just as soon set fire to. But he couldn't go the distance in any way, shape or form. Truth is, he's afraid.

He remembers too well sitting in the driveway holding on to the wheel for dear life, but doesn't remember Francey getting in beside him, her face frozen in disbelief that he was the one losing it. The doctor's verdict delivered, they had both had the instinct to run away, literally, right then. They sat in the Honda in the driveway staring at the windshield that only looked onto the back wall of the carport at the unused tools hanging on hooks, the unfinished projects cluttering the workbench. A cradle, for one, a box without rockers. After a long while, he looked over at her, hoping she could see he was a man who still had the bearing of someone who had once defied gravity, no matter how briefly. It was his most ardent wish he might, in some way, do so again.

And now, trudging through this new emptiness, his flawed body is the only thing he has left. He's brought no water, no knapsack, not even a stick of gum. It's just him and his feet, moving mechanically, a forced march under hot sun. Thank God it's only February, and he does have a map in his back pocket. But still, the sun is blinding here, penetrating. Blades of light drill deep into his head. A quote by Beckett he used to keep over his desk beats inside him like a metronome, a rhythm he walks to. "I can't go on. I'll go on." He does. He does. He does.

His own breathing is weirdly magnified as if he were inside a diving bell, counting down the number of breaths allotted to him in this life. His heart, unaccustomed to so much beating, becomes a fist knocking on a closed door. Behind that door, the fear of losing everything. This fragile, new idea of himself. What he can be now that he can't be what he'd always wanted to become? He's nobody's father. What he wanted, maybe even more than the child, was to show his own father how it could, how it should be done.

His father had tricked him once. Only once, when he was five. Told him to jump off the side of the pool at the Y, that he would catch him. But as soon as Rooney jumped, his father lowered his arms, moved aside and Rooney plunged into water way over his head, flailing. He opened his eyes and saw his father's legs, his feet firmly planted on the bottom of the pool, his bathing trunks ballooning over hairy thighs. Rooney came up for air. Sink or swim, his father said, and laughed. Rooney didn't sink. He didn't swim, either. But he remained suspended in shame for eternity.

In an eerie twist of fate, his father had a stroke and subsisted, if that's what you can call it, in a chronic vegetative state in a nursing home in Tyler. Five whole years in a body without a mind suspended between two worlds, neither of which would have him.

That's his own greatest fear, Rooney realizes now. That suspension, that inability to go forward or back. But here, in the desert, there's only one direction: toward the hot springs. Toward the woman he loves and two people who could become good friends in good time. He's exhausted but he keeps on.

At the turnoff to Solis landing he sees two men with heavy sacks, their clothes wet from crossing the river. Then he hears shots, near him, very near him. He isn't sure where the shots are coming from, who they're meant for. Maybe they're meant for him. He feels a sense of real danger, the physical kind that involves weapons, motives, international grudges, and broken treaties. Here he is, a gringo—there's no other word for it—bumbling into things that are really none of his business. He breaks into a stumbling run.

He could disappear now so easily, into Mexico where he would have to relearn everything, like a man with aphasia. Harry Dean Stanton had had to grow into a man, become the father, but Rooney would descend now, fall all the way into becoming a boy—a weightless, fatherless boy who could fly on his own.

Canyon wrens call out to each other, their voices like notes from a wooden flute echoing off the canyon walls alongside him. His legs move, a running trudge. He stumbles on a rock, falls forward from an embankment, hands first toward a wash six feet below.

For a full second he's flying, his body borne on an updraft of heated air. The fall, when it comes this time, is soft, in deep mud that he sinks into, feet first, then tips forward on all fours, sliding until he's stretched out, face down, water flowing not five feet away.

He stays like that, afraid to move at first, listening for the pain that comes from broken bones. The shame of injury. He moves his legs. No pain. He flexes his hands. He's okay.

He crawls out of the mud, a newborn amphibious creature, whose gills evolve quickly into lungs. His new legs bear his weight. He turns, looks back at the mud, at the splayed impression his body made. He looks down at his feet. He moves the left foot first. Then the right. He can walk. Yes, walk. He can go faster. Trot. Further on, he can run, really run, his body not foe now, but friend.

He starts to slow down, to listen. He comes closer, hears the sound of laughter, of bodies in water. He doesn't know if this is an auditory hallucination or not. It's Francey, her voice low and sonorous. He hears Tim's voice now. This isn't a dream. He's found them. He actually covered what looked like an enormous distance on the map. He ran farther than he realized, farther than he ever thought he could.

He could call out. But he doesn't. Will he see something that his physical presence would render invisible? Something he needs to see?

He finds a good vantage point, a thick covering of tamarisk and reeds. He disappears into it, parts it ever so slightly. And there, in what's left of the hot springs, sits the woman he loves, lolling in water up to her waist. She's leaning back in the corner of a concrete bath. Even in the waning light he can see her ample thighs ripple, luminous as pearl in the water, her nipples shockingly huge and hard beneath her blue tank suit. Tim and Annie sit close together. Behind them, what's left of the Rio Grande trickles down from El Paso. And just beyond this narrow, liquid border sitting on their heels by a smoking fire are the Mexicans. Boys and young men. A couple of dogs. Are they here to watch the gringos in bathing suits? Or are they loading their guns, preparing to cross over, to deliver something or someone to a courier?

There are at least eight of them.

He watches these young men, these young boys closely. Their faces look so dark, almost brooding. But not dangerous.

Tim and Annie and Francey all have their backs to Mexico. They can't see these people and their fire. Or maybe they already have and think nothing of it.

Should he warn them? No, he'll watch until—until what? What's he going to do if they start shooting—come charging out of the bushes brandishing a rock? Or let it happen—whatever it is that's going to happen now that he's here, now that he's a different person, now that the truth of many things feels so much closer at hand.

One of the boys—a young man, really—gets up from his crouched position, walks over to a pile of something, and picks up an armload of sticks. Rooney thinks he's about to stoke the fire, but he walks into the water, his pants soaking like a wick almost to his knees. He starts to come across.

The boy holds up the sticks. "Five," he says to the three Americans sitting in the water. "Five dollars. Last time."

The sticks are carved, painted with animals. Rooney can see the colors from here, even in the fading light. Hieroglyphics of a simpler life. Half a day of labor. Five dollars. The boy's pants are soaked. The sun's almost gone and the air quickly grows colder.

Francey waves the boy over. Tim's found some money in the pocket of his shorts. Wet, but still legal tender. She stands up, dripping, the water that's been inside her running down her thighs.

The boy stops halfway across the river, and for the first time Rooney sees how vulnerable this boy actually is. He could get shot from *this* side. The Border Patrol on the mountain behind him. A vigilante for Homeland Security who doesn't know the difference between an Arab and a Mexican, taking the law into his own hands.

Rooney stands up, pushing apart the dry reeds, crashing through.

The boy drops the sticks and runs. The rest of his people on the other side scatter, disappear into the thicket through the reeds.

Annie lurches in the water trying to stand up. Tim turns around abruptly, wet dollars in his hand.

Francey turns, her hand flies to her chest. "You scared me!"

she cries out to Rooney when she sees him. "Are you all right? We've been worried!"

He can't answer any of it. He's hasn't learned how to speak yet. The walking sticks the boy dropped bunch together into a small log jam, then slowly, one frees itself, slides downriver, then another, and another. Something else he dropped catches in an eddy, frees itself, and floats toward him.

Tim looks at Rooney curiously. "They thought you were *La Migra*, the Border Patrol." It's apparent to everyone now that they've been watched, that Rooney has been here—for how long and why—hiding in the reeds?

"Rooney?" Francey says, as if she's not sure it's him.

The last thing he wanted to do was scare anyone. What had he wanted? He looks at her, and she him. Something passes between them, a silence filled with private knowledge of what can break a man, or anyone. Of what can stir him again.

What the boy dropped floats toward him, bobbing—a jar with a lid. Rooney reaches down and picks it up. There's something inside.

He unscrews the lid, takes out a piece of paper and reads it in the last of the light. It's in all capital letters, a little downhill, but readable. English.

The people of Boquillas ask for you help. We have nothing now. We are grateful for any giving. We thank you from the depth of our hearts.

Rooney raises his eyes from the paper. He can feel them watching, the people of Boquillas across the river. The messenger? But there was no question. Still, some kind of answer is required.

Rooney takes out his billfold. There's at least a hundred there, plus the twenty he'd folded in his pocket to put in the envelope for camping at La Kiva.

Rooney puts it all in the jar. All. And he knows it isn't nearly enough.

He steps into the river, his wet shoes still on, his muddy jeans growing darker blue at the bottom. He wades out toward the middle and stops. The water comes to his knees. He lifts his arm, holds up the jar. The river flows around him, the line between his country and theirs a black, unstoppable blur.

Tim and Annie and Francey stand on the shore behind him. Nobody says anything. Just the river now, going on and on.

Slowly, very slowly, the boy comes out of the reeds and stands at the edge. He looks out at Rooney, the jar. A trick? A gift?

Rooney starts toward him. The boy raises his hand, palm out for him to stop. The boy knows exactly where the line is.

The boy comes into the river, to the place he knows for certain is the center. He stops. Rooney leans forward with the jar. The boy takes it in his left hand. As they watch, the boy places his right hand over his heart and holds it there.

Rooney can feel the line between here and there, a definite edge between plenty and enough. Between want and need. Now all he has to do is fall the rest of the way. Head first into the world where he's been headed all along. But all Rooney can do is listen to his own pounding heart.

The boy and the man are turning in different directions, walking out of the same river without a word, just the sound of their feet in the water, the silence as they reach dry land of different countries.

On one side of the river, desperate people. Whom Rooney has helped, at least a little. On this side, the woman he loves and still wants, who will need something else from him now.

Steam rises out of the roof vent of the Love Bug. Francey sits on the small bed with Annie, cross-legged, facing each other. There's a pot boiling on the stove, the pungent smell of sage permeating the air.

Annie scrutinizes the tarot cards Francey pulled from the deck. The Hanged Man. An upside-down figure, a benign, accepting smile on his face.

"Surrender," Annie says. "You have to get turned upside down to see things straight." All morning she's heard Francey's story. All of it.

"Ah," says Francey. "I see." And she does. It's her, all right, hanging from the crosspiece. Not Rooney. Surrender. All she can associate with that is "Surrender Dorothy" in the *Wizard of Oz*. Skywriting by a witch. But it isn't to the witch she needs to surrender. It's the story. The story about reward for trying so hard. Acceptance was something other people talked about, other people who didn't have anything crucial they needed to let go of. She didn't know how *not* to try. She was a tryer from a way back. Straight A's, always. A career as a legal assistant, good at separating other people's facts and fictions. But she couldn't conceive. And she'd tried so hard. Too hard, maybe. But it's not the child now. It's her conception about herself that needs to be surrendered.

"Give it up," Annie says, turning the cards over, putting them into a pile again.

"Easy for you to say."

"No. It isn't."

Annie looks at her curiously, then her face settles into certainty, as if she's just found the key she was looking for.

"Did you try to have children?" Francey asks.

"No. I never did."

"Have them or try to have them?"

"Neither. I never really wanted children. I wanted freedom. I have freedom. Isn't that what you want, too?"

Francey ignores the question. Her sense of freedom comes and goes. Only yesterday, she was soaring. Today she feels like she made a crash landing. "So what did you try *not* to do?"

Annie looks at her, her gaze level, her hands resting comfortably in her lap. "I just stopped trying to change Tim into somebody else."

"And did it work, the not trying?"

"He changed anyway. It's his story."

"Story?"

"Getting clean."

"He got sober?"

"He'd be dead if he wasn't."

"He seems happy."

"He is. Every day is a new day, or so he says."

"You believe him?"

"It doesn't matter if I do or not. He does."

"And what do you believe in?"

"It depends on when you ask. Sometimes it's that shit happens. Right now it's that anything can happen, and that includes good things."

"I was raised to roll up my sleeves. My dad had a Damn Yankee mentality. That's how things got done in my family," Francey says.

"And your mom?"

"She capitulated with dignity."

"Maybe that's why things got done."

"I don't see it that way."

"Of course not. That's why you're sitting here with me reading tarot cards."

"Touché." She uncrosses her legs, draws her knees up, holds them with her arms.

"What about *us*?" Francey says.

"What *about* us?"

"Now what? Now that *they* have their bearings."

"We get ours back," Annie says.

"Just like that," Francey says testily. "I really don't need a one day at a time lecture now."

"It's less than that."

"Less than what?"

"A day's way too long."

Francey looks at Annie directly, searching for malice, but there is none, only the wear and tear of wisdom.

She thinks about the old man who ran a hotel in Mineola, where she grew up. Hardly anybody ever came to the hotel so the old man spent his time sitting in the lobby painting, which was what he really wanted to do anyway. Wild horses in arroyos. Lonely cowboys leaning into the wind. She used to spend hours just watching him stroke color onto canvas, bringing out what was shimmering there just behind the blank white square. He said, on her seventh birthday, "Miss Francey, I'm going to give you a gift, a secret. Life is like this: You put in your order for what you want and what you order comes back. Order happiness, well, you get happiness. Order misery and doubt, well, that's what comes back." She pictured heaven as a diner, the Heart's Desire Diner. Waitresses taking your order, sticking them on the little wheel by the kitchen, spinning it. Order up! Over the years she'd ordered up a shitload of doubt and plain old unadulterated fear. Fear that there wasn't enough of anything. That she'd give everything she had and be left holding the bag, bitter and barren and alone.

She picks up the card of the Hanged Man to look more closely. He doesn't look frightened at his position. He seems to be gazing serenely at the oak from which he's dangling, as if he's never seen such a beautiful tree in his life.

"Go fish," Annie says, holding out the deck.

Francey draws another. The Fool. A youth happily traveling, looking at the sky, about to fall off a cliff.

"Ah," Annie says.

"What?"

"You're in for a surprise. Whatever you do, don't look before you leap."

Rooney and Tim scan the notices flapping in the wind tacked to a board outside the Study Butte grocery store and gas station. Swamp coolers. Puppies. A winch. Yoga lessons. Rooney finds one index card, half hidden. *10 Acres. $1,000. Gate One and a Half.* He does a double take. There's a phone number. He shows it to Tim.

"Go for it," Tim says. "If you don't, I will."

Rooney dials the number on Tim's cell phone. A man answers on the second ring.

"Yes."

Not hello, not yes, raised as a question, but as a statement, as if they've already agreed.

"I saw your ad," Rooney says.

"Which one?"

"About the land."

"Yeah. I'm also selling a bass amp."

"I don't need a bass amp. I'm calling about the land."

"What about it?"

"Well, can you describe it?"

"It's desert, mister."

"I realize that . . ."

"We don't have anything else around here. No palm trees. No lagoons. No Club Med on the horizon."

"I can see that."

Silence on the other end of the line. A crackling as if the telephone line is a lit fuse slowly burning.

Tim searches through a box of free clothes on a bench, holding up an orange striped shirt. Too small. He puts it back.

"So where's Gate One and a Half?" Rooney pictures an entrance, a legitimate entrance flanked by stone lions.

"Where are *you?*" the man says.

"I'm staying at La Kiva."

"Rancho Borracho," the man says. Rooney laughs. He remembers the Loteria card for borracho—the drunk holding a bottle, reeling.

"Are you there now? They don't have a working phone."

"No, I'm at Study Butte store."

"Stoody, not Study. Gate One and a Half is a couple of miles north of where you're standing."

Tim tries on a bowler hat. Too big. It covers his eyes. He gives a little Chaplin kick.

Rooney turns, tethered by the silver cord to the phone. "All I can see is some kind of mountain."

"Bee Mountain. Past that."

"I can't see past that from here. Can I come and look at it?"

"Go ahead."

"Can you give me some directions?" Rooney's really getting irritated now. More Terlingua double-talk. That's the third language implied by the name, not Comanche.

"Have you got a GPS?"

"A what?"

"Global Positioning Device."

"Hardly. Are you there—at the land?"

"No. I live behind the store where you're standing."

"How come you're selling it?"

"I'm not selling the store."

"I mean the *land.* I'm calling about the *land.*"

Tim leaves the box of clothes and comes toward Rooney.

"Back taxes."

"Is that a lot? I mean, the price seems, well . . ." He doesn't want to use the word cheap. He covers the phone, looks at Tim. "It's a steal," he says. He speaks into the phone again. "Are the taxes unusually high down here?"

"Well, that's what I owe. Ten years of back taxes."

"*Ten years!*"

"It's a long time," the voice says. "I can see that now."

"Look," Rooney says. "Can you take me and my friend there? Meet us here. Now?"

"Do you have a car?"

"We walked."

The man laughs. "We'll take my van."

"We'll wait right here."

"Twenty minutes."

"I thought you said you lived right behind the store."

"It'll take me that long to get the van started."

Rooney hangs up the phone and turns to Tim. "I don't know if this is too good to be true or not."

"Well, just remember, it's off the grid. You'll have to figure out a twelve-volt system, water catchment . . ."

"I could do that," Rooney says. "I really could."

Tim looks at Rooney, smiles. "I don't have any doubts. You look like somebody who steps up to the plate."

"How's that?"

"You just stepped right out there in the river last night. I was wondering what to do while you just went ahead and did it."

"I didn't think."

"Exactly. I was. About getting busted by the Border Patrol."

A van with expired tags pulls up, sputtering. A man in a black cowboy hat with a hawk feather stuck in the band, a stampede strap dangling below his chin leans out the window. His hair is pulled back in a long ponytail.

"Get in," he says.

Rooney opens the passenger door that grinds horribly on its hinges. He climbs in, hauling himself up by a handle bolted onto the dash. It takes both hands to pull the door closed. Tim climbs in back. The van is built like a tank. There's a PA in the back and about fifty plastic jugs of water, a shovel, a pickaxe. A sleeping bag. A can of sterno and a coffee pot.

"Name's Jerry," the man says. "This is my home sweet home."

"Rooney."

"Rooney what?"

"Jensen. And this is Tim . . ." He realizes he doesn't know his last name.

Tim doesn't offer it. Surnames are for anywhere else but here.

"Jerry what?"

"Clockwork Cowboy."

"You're kidding."

"That's what they call me around here."

"How come?"

"Beats me. Hang around here long enough they'll start calling you something, too, Walking Bob, Pablo Menudo . . ."

"What do you do—some kind of masonry or something?" Tim says.

"I used to be a bass player. Now I play the banjo. Doesn't require electricity. Have you got a couple of bucks for gas?"

"Sure," Rooney says, reaching for his wallet. He and Tim exchange a complicit glance. This could be a great deal. This guy's desperate.

"Preciate it. Haven't had a decent gig in a while."

"I got a banjo joke," Tim says.

"Who doesn't?" Jerry says, checking him out in the rearview mirror.

"What's worse than two banjoes?" Tim asks. He pauses, then says. "Nothing."

Silence from Jerry. Then he actually laughs.

Rooney starts to give him a five, then adds another, glad he has the money from the sale of the house. This van won't get far on five.

Jerry puts five in the tank, pockets the rest. Then they're off to Gate One and a Half, past Bee Mountain, north on 118 toward Alpine.

"First time here?" he asks Rooney.

"Yeah. Lived in Texas my whole life and didn't get here until yesterday."

"Lot of people say that. It's not on the way to anywhere except off the edge of the world. Some people come to visit and get stuck here. Terlingua Triangle, we call it. How did you get here?" he asks Tim.

"My wife and I were on our way to Tucson and took a detour. About a month ago. Feels like forever. I mean, in a good way. What about you?"

"Heard about it when I was up in Montana working on a fire crew one summer. A guy in Bozeman told me. I won the land in a poker game. I don't play anymore. Anyway," he says, "we loaded up in his Bonneville and booked on down here. He said there wasn't any law down here, that you could get stoned and stay that way and play music all day long. I said, 'hell, let's go.' And here I am. That was ten years ago."

He makes an abrupt left turn into an unpaved road. There's no gate that Rooney can see. The van careens around a sharp down-hill turn then lurches through the deep rut of a dry streambed, nearly bogging down in sand.

Rooney holds onto the handle on the dashboard with both hands as the van bucks its way up the far bank. Tim rolls against the side of the van, grabbing the bass amp for balast. The road winds back and forth sharply around low gray hills bunched like a school of whales stranded in sand. Further on, the velvet gray whales morph into dinosaurs, their backs ridged with lava scree. Countless dry streambeds criss-cross the road and there's many places where tire tracks have left a deep impression, crusted and baked in the sun. Hardly any vegetation. A few brave prickly pear, a single ocotillo, and a solitary boulder in the curved flank of a hill like a Zen garden after a nuclear blast. No wonder it's cheap. And yet, it's weirdly beautiful in a Cro-Magnon kind of way, the bones of the earth revealing their mysterious shapes, a preview for the film of the beginning of creation, without any soundtrack but the high-lonesome wind.

In twenty minutes they've gone a mile and a half. Jerry nego-tiates a particularly treacherous sinkhole between two high dirt dikes. An entryway of sorts.

"Is this Gate One and a Half?" Rooney asks.

"The whole thing is Gate One and a Half. Bentonite Central."
Jerry waves his arm at the considerable expanse.

"What's bentonite?"

"They seal ponds with it. It's kitty litter, too."

"No way."

"No, really," Tim says. "It's what they make it from. Gray clay."

Jerry stops the van. Or did it simply die? Halfway up a hillside are the remnants of several vehicles. A school bus. A Dodge Valiant. A Ford 250 on blocks.

"This is it," Jerry says, his arm sweeping a wide arc encompassing a mountain, a mesa. "Halfway up that mountain there—see that mesquite scrub—there might be a spring."

"Might be?"

"I been digging it out for a couple of years now in my free time. I'm close, real close. Get you some PVC and a stock tank and you'll be all set. Catching rain is a pain in the ass."

"What about a well?"

"That's one expensive screw. Iffy, to boot." Jerry lights up a joint, passes it to Tim. Tim looks at it a long time, studying the curl of smoke from its ragged end. He passes it straight to Rooney without taking a drag.

It's been a long time. So long it's like the first time—that mangled looking bony white finger pointed at him, offered, pinched between thumb and forefinger. Rooney takes it. What the hell. This guy could be the messenger he's been waiting for. Don Juan's prodigal son. And Rooney a new millennium Carlos Castenada willing to cross the threshold to the real mystery, to have his head opened up, the shit scooped out and a beautiful emptiness poured in, an emptiness with a reflective quality capable not only of perceiving truth but instilling in him the willingness to live by it.

But he doesn't take a drag on the joint. He hands it back to Jerry. He's already reeling from some chemical change in his head—something he hasn't felt in a long time. Enthusiasm. Hope. It's intoxicating. He feels the earth shift on its axis, the sky stretch beyond his peripheral vision. He turns around for the 360-degree view. Jerry goes on about something or other—wind generators, infinite chord combinations based on the I Ching, the intricate architecture of Brian Wilson's *Smile* album. Then he's opening up the back of his van, wrestling with the huge speakers of the PA, sliding them to the edge of the tailgate, putting that very CD into a player that's wired to a 12V battery spitting sparks like something in a science project, a laboratory in a horror film.

He jumps out of the van and beckons. Rooney and Tim follow. Upward, on a hacked-out path, the swelling crescendo of twelve-part harmony not only ricochets off the mesa but bores into it so that they're not so much listening to the music as climbing through it. Up to the top of the mesa, winded, they meet the wind, a force to be leaned into as it plays the spindly strings of the ocotillo, plucks their own bodies like thick, flat-wound bass strings. Brian Wilson's voice is like Jesus in the wilderness backed up by a choir of lost souls, illegal immigrants, orphans, soaring out of longing into the light of the upper world. Two ravens glide into the mix, squawking. The mountain range to the southeast has just now risen out of tectonic friction, dripping with magma, the clouds above them steam meeting the cooler air. Wilson got it. Gets it. The real rapture is right here, right now for the true believers, not pulled naked into heaven, but to the epiphany on earth where the wind and sun converge and a man takes his rightful place among creatures, not over them, giving up dominion for being a part of it all. The Creator's leftover rock pile is the perfect place to begin.

This is it. Where he belongs. The fact that he has enough money in his pocket to buy it feels incredible.

"I'll take it!" he says to Jerry. Jerry doesn't hear over this thunderous version of "Good Vibrations." It's coming not out of the van, but out of the ground, as if it's just now being born from raw materials. Sound rolls like a typhoon, cresting the mesa and continuing on, unimpeded by anything made by man.

"I'll take it," he says again, in the brief segue between songs.

"Whoa!" Tim says, not in caution, but in appreciation. "Dude!" and claps Rooney on the shoulder.

Jerry smiles. A Cheshire Cat in a hat. Wilson's pilgrim. "You won't regret it, man," he says. "Believe me." But there's a sadness when he says it. He coughs. "I kissed the ground when I first got here," he says. "But I can't stand to kiss it goodbye. I was going to do something with it. Build something, you know? I didn't know jack about building. I'm a musician. But at least I know who's getting it. Who'll take care of it and not sell it to some developer from Dallas."

Ten acres surrounded by thousands. It doesn't matter where the boundaries are. There aren't any. Not another human structure in sight and the contrail from a jet high above doesn't even scratch the surface of the sky. It's vast. Leviathan. Better than ocean. You can *walk* on it. You can sit on it, which Rooney does right now, collapsing to his knees. You can lie down on it, which is easy. Just a rocking to the left, then a roll, his legs stretching out, Gulliver's shoes hanging over the edge of the world. The sky pulls on his face. He lets it stretch him. He falls upward into it, arms out. The ravens squawk as they catch him between four wings, bearing him into the wild blue.

A face looms over him in a black hat, blocking the sun. Bob Dylan on the cover of Nashville Skyline with a Mona Lisa smile.

"So?" the face says.

Rooney blinks. What a perfect question.

He rolls to the side, reaches in his back pocket for his wallet. It's there. He pulls out ten one hundred dollar travelers checks. Hermes in a helmet presiding.

He hands them over.

"You have to sign them," Tim says.

"Details, details," Rooney says. "I don't have a pen." He laughs. He'll sign it in blood if need be. It's the first transaction he's made in his life where he feels truly happy. Home. They'll stay here. He'll find water with his own two hands. Maybe she'll even admire him again. Maybe he'll admire himself for a change.

Tim has found a pen somehow and Rooney sits up, using his knee as a desk. Ten times he writes his name and there's an evolution in it, a kind of dissolving from perfect penmanship to scrawl, a freedom in the letters of his name once they don't have to be particularly legible. His mark in the brand-new world.

He hands the checks to Tim. Tim passes them to Jerry, who pockets them. Jerry turns slowly counterclockwise, taking it all in, what he's about to leave. To Rooney's amazement, there are tears in Jerry's eyes when he completes the circle. "I'm going to miss this place, man," he says. "Take good care of it. Please." He heads back down the hill to the van.

Tim holds out his hand toward Rooney to pull him up. Rooney takes it and there's a feeling of sealing the bargain, man to man, not with Jerry but with Tim. After all, they found it together. Maybe he and Annie will bring the Love Bug out here, at least for a while.

Tim pulls. Rooney rises. There's a moment where each fights to regain his balance. Tim lets go of him and Rooney stands there, rocking on his feet, standing on his land, a little pushpin on an enormous map. You are Here. And he is. After all these years.

"I envy you, man," Tim says.

"Why? I thought you were the intrepid one."

"Who said that?"

"I just see you that way. I did from the get-go," Rooney says.

"Yeah, well, maybe I'm a good faker. What you just did took considerable balls."

"What do you mean?"

"Well, you didn't ask Francey, did you? But then, maybe you know her, inside and out."

Rooney shakes his head. "I thought I did. I couldn't give her what she wanted."

"What does she need instead?"

Rooney looks at Tim. He's always asking him questions he doesn't seem to be able to answer. He shakes his head. "I'm not sure now."

"Well, you're about to find out." Tim reaches in his pocket, hands something to Rooney. "My lucky guitar pick," he says. "It's silver. You might need it."

"I can't take that," Rooney says.

"Sure you can," Tim says and slides it into Rooney's shirt pocket. On his face Rooney sees a man who, besides his certainty and dexterity with musical instruments, still relies on something he can't easily explain.

"Some serious mojo in there," Tim says, indicating the Love Bug, which now seems more like a curandera's crucible than a travel trailer. "We could use some of that ourselves. But I suspect that if a group of men got together we wouldn't do much of anything but whittle and argue."

Rooney laughs. "Naw. You and I would be stirring up some interesting trouble somewhere, somehow." He high-fives Tim. "Can I borrow your truck for a little while to take Francey out there?"

"Sure," Tim says. "There's plenty of gas in it."

Rooney knocks on the door to the Love Bug. Annie and Francey don't answer.

Rooney opens the door. "I've got something to show you. You won't believe it."

"What is it?"

"You'll see."

Francey looks at Annie, who's got an "I told you so" look on her face. For half a second, she feels a fleeting complicity with her. Now she's about to leave that feminine solidarity in the Love Bug and head out for who knows what. Surrender. Pay attention. Well, she can at least do that.

"Come with me," he says to Francey, opening the passenger door to the Toyota gallantly.

Francey gets in, casts a look back at Annie. Rooney can't see Francey's face but he can see Annie as she looks at Francey. Where do they get that intuition from? It's frightening, the way they seem to summon it, telepathically. Annie looks at him now, the hunch growing. As if she could even guess.

"So what is this surprise?" Francey says, buckling herself in.

"You'll see."

"Why can't you just tell me?" she says.

"Because it wouldn't be a surprise."

She can buy that. But she also knows there's power in with-holding. She doesn't even know why she's thinking like this, why she's feeling so irritated.

"Well, I've had about all the surprises I can stand."

"Come on, Francey."

"No—you come on. You wear me out, Rooney. You really do. You disappear for half a day, lose the Vespa, and I worry you've wound up dead somewhere. God knows what you've gotten into now."

"Trust me, Francey."

"Why should I?"

"Because I'm finally asking you to."

She looks at him, his hands on the wheel. This is new, this ask-ing. And there's other things that are new—that giveaway in the river last night. She'd been moved. It wasn't like him to step so far forward. Still, she didn't know where it came from, that gesture. *What about me?* she wants to say. But she's no whiner. She'll wait and see, for now.

Clouds pile up behind Bee Mountain, marching down from Marfa. The sun ducks behind them and stays there. Francey grabs for the dashboard as the Toyota careens down the turnoff road from Highway 118. Felipe, the smiling skeleton, dangles from the rearview mirror, guitar in hand, swinging wildly. Rooney navigates the switchbacks, the dry creeks, the cavernous potholes. He and Tim marked the forks with cairns on his way out with Jerry, know-ing he'd get lost otherwise. There's a warren of roads back here.

Still, they might get in there and never get out. Be picked apart by vultures and scorpions. Or cleared of doubt and earthly apathy and trepidation. Deserts can do that—kill you. Or cure you.

He drives past their disappointment at the first fork, onward toward their now prehistoric hope, each turn leaving a decade behind. That's the way it feels to him, driving, both hands on the wheel. History unravels behind them like a pulled thread that snagged somewhere back on pavement, somewhere on the nail of a vow. And where are they when the truck comes to a stop on a small slope bordered by a mountain and a mesa with a staggering sweep of sky? Adolescence, at least, where they're capable of wonder, all the rest quelled by a grandeur that dares any doubt to rear its ugly head.

There's a different frequency in the air. She can feel it. Francey lets herself barely begin to imagine it: a chance. A chance where they might meet all over again. In the American outback. The final frontier: relationship. Where everyone has boldly gone before.

Rooney shuts off the engine.

"Happy birthday," he says.

"Oh, you shouldn't have," she says. "It's not my birthday. What are you talking about?"

"It's yours. Ours."

"What is? The Toyota?" She considers a karmic exchange—the Vespa for the Toyota. Fair enough.

"This," he says, getting out of the truck, leaving the door open, the key in the ignition, a bell chiming to remind him not to lock himself out.

She takes the keys out. Drops them in the seat. "You're kidding." She steps out of the truck, leaning on the open door.

"Tell me you're kidding."

He comes around to her side. "I've never been more serious in my life. I bought ten acres for a mere one thousand dollars."

He grabs her hand and pulls. She stays rooted to the spot. A hundred things go through her head.

"What are we going to do with this?"

"We don't have to do anything. It's not a fixer-upper. I bought it 'as is.'" He grins.

"You do things without thinking of what effect they'll have on anyone else. There is no anyone else when you've got an idea. It's like an alarm goes off and your brain drowns out anything else until you can complete the thought and shut the alarm off."

She wishes she didn't know all this, that there was still some of that sixties emotional amnesia, caution thrown to the wind because the magical mystery tour bus might finally be about to leave and she really doesn't want to be left behind.

"Is that how you think of me?" he asks.

"No, that's how I feel. Sometimes. Now."

"So what do you think?"

"I think you're out of your mind."

"Once upon a time you liked that. Said that you missed it. Well, here it is. Here we are. Come on, Francey. It's not too late. Play with me."

What can she order up from the Heart's Desire Diner? Maybe they've finally run out of defeat. She looks at the face of her husband, flushed with excitement, with this surprise, this gift he wants to give her, even if it seems outrageous. In truth, she wants it more than she can say.

There's a moon, fuller than the other night above the mountains, breaking through cloud cover above the Chisos. Fuchsia dusk pervades the mountains. There are no pastels here. The sky, the part that isn't cloudy, is still a brazen blue, deepening to shades that have yet to be named. The ocotillo stalks sway wildly in the rising wind, raking the air around them.

He turns to look at her when they reach the top. "See?" he says. "Do you see?"

She nods her head slowly, taking it all in, flooded with conflicting feelings she's powerless to suppress. Does any of this really include her? Is this what love looks like, this gift? Is this what love feels like, this wonder at the person before you who surprises and irritates you, at your own self for being surprised and irritated, but abiding, after all? In a backdrop of spindly flora, rooted in rock, thriving in arid country because it knows in every cell that rain, though it cannot be counted on, will someday surely come?

Rooney lets go of her hand, holding both arms out, not just toward her, but toward all of it, including her, and he's turning as if the wind is unwinding him. Then he's walking through the ocotillo forest, exploring, picking up small stones that catch his eye, trusting her to be there when he returns, or to follow if she wants to. He's found his element and he's in it. A man who walked into a river and bought a piece of the earth for a song.

She's never felt more connected, never felt more alone.

Crimson go the clouds. Magnolia white, the moon. Her husband is running, propelled by a joy she didn't know he was capable of. A lovable boy, not the difficult, thwarted man. And what kind of woman is she now? She holds her hands out in front of her, palms up, turns them over. Roots, not veins. Roots leading to the stump of her heart. Is it still there? She unbuttons her shirt. Takes it off. Lets the wind caress her exposed breasts. Steps out of her jeans. Her black underwear. All of it ending up in a pile next to her feet, her gleaming gold toes. A girl, visible under the broad, reckless sky.

All her flaws and imperfections of fast-approaching middle age: the cellulite, the rolls and bulges she's kept under wraps. On her upturned face, the first few drops of rain. Let him look. The Creator, if there is one; Rooney, if he can.

Rooney's not running now, he's walking slowly toward her. He stops ten feet away.

His eyes rest their gaze on belly. Higher, at the breasts, her breasts, at the nipples, hardening. To tell the truth, which he must, from here on in, she looks absolutely gorgeous in the rarified, creosote-scented air of Terlingua. He stands before her, his belly sagging, his penis rising. Effortlessly. It seems, if he could move inside her, that he will be stirring her, concocting something. That's what her vagina might say: stir thoroughly and let sit. Preheat oven to high. Isn't it time for sex to have a little humor? Is there a Loteria card for it, this place he could find himself inside? *La vagina?* A dark mouth opening onto mystery.

The ovaries, still on their stalks, are making eggs anyway, but fewer every year. The last one could very well be making its way this moment toward that empty cave where there is nothing left to cling to. Where, this second, her husband approaches the mouth of it. She takes his hand, places it there, between her legs. He closes his eyes. He doesn't move.

Then his fingers do, searching toward a hidden spring. She grabs his hand, brings it to her mouth. Tastes that blank, infinitesimal embryo on the tip of her tongue.

She shivers. From all of it. The change in the air, the coming storm. The change in herself, and him. Lightning punctuates everything now, his face before her stark white. Scared? Or just illuminated? She leans against him. He, her.

His body is solid, still. Flesh on the bones, his heart a hard muscle. Thunder. The sky opens in a perfect reprieve. He takes off his jacket, puts it around her. A high school gesture. Sweet. Sweeter. She grabs her clothes and shoes and they rush toward the edge of the mesa, the edge of the world. On her bare soles she can feel it, sharpness giving way to soft, the earth melting with every step. Her body melting with every step. She sinks deeper. By the time they slog their way downhill, water pours off the mesa behind them, filling the path. By the time they reach the truck her feet sink in at least two inches of mud, making wonderfully sexual, sucking sounds with each step. Rooney trudges in shoes caked in mud. They look like the bulbous appendages on Felipe, the dashboard skeleton.

They get in the truck. Pull the doors closed, roll up the windows, breathing hard.

They look at each other in a lightning flash. Should they laugh?

Here she sits, naked, a jacket around her shoulders like an awkward virgin at a drive-in movie, her sex sticky with anticipation, primed.

He starts up the truck, revving it. They have to hurry. He's had first-hand experience with this mud. He puts the truck in gear, steps on the gas, and the wheels spin crazily while the truck slithers and turns slowly around. They're headed downhill now and the truck picks up speed, skidding to the left. Rooney hits the brakes, and they slide completely off the road. There's no stopping it. There isn't much of a hill but it's slick, the mud the consistency of Crisco. No dropoff, no cliff, just this long slow skid, mowing down prickly pear as they go.

Instinct makes him throw out his right arm to protect her. Their voices raise an octave as they scream, "Oh, no!" climaxing in a collective shriek as the truck meets the melting, earthen dike with a soft thud just to the left of where the road cuts through. The Toyota, finally meeting resistance, has come to rest, relatively unscathed like a piece of flotsam, and the river the road has become rushes past, under the wheels, out through the gate between the two dikes into the bentonite flats beyond.

"Jesus Christ," Rooney says. "Wow."

Francey feels a seismic rumble, laughter coming up through her belly, her lungs, out of her mouth. They're stuck, literally and completely. She holds up both hands in surrender.

They'll have to walk all the way back to La Kiva, explain to Tim and Annie. Pray for sun to dry the mud so they can get the Toyota out. *Mañana. Mañana.* What's the hurry any more? There's all the time in the world to stop trying.

The rain stops as suddenly as it began. The moon floats, surveying the spectacle below. An uncharted river, receding even as it flows. A jackrabbit emerges from behind a rock, ears picking up the breathing of the two humans nearby. A tiny truck, doors opening like wings now. A chiming sound. Headlights illuminate the rock, the rabbit, then they extinguish. A hand reaches up, switches off the dome light; the chiming stops. A ratcheting sound as the parking brake is set. A tiny skeleton swings from the rearview mirror, facing his audience of two.

It's hard to say which of them moves first. Hands float toward each other and fold together. The heads lean toward each other until they touch, not face to face, but at the side. Ear to ear. A meeting of the minds. Listening. The bodies simmer far below.

What are they thinking?

The moon takes a closer look, looming through the windshield, free of all clouds. The woman throws a piece of clothing out the open door. She is naked and made of soft, white marble. The man is still fully clothed, rumpled. But not for long. He takes off his muddy shoes, throws them both out the window. She unbuttons his shirt. Unbuckles his belt and pulls.

A little figurine swings slowly back and forth from the rearview mirror, watching as the bodies, shed of clothing, make a bed of a reclining bucket seat and move together, breathing like runners who have paced themselves and are now going for the gold, though silver would do them just fine.

After a time, the figurine slows its swinging, comes to a stop. Breathing slows, thoughts return. Postcoital thinking, in lieu of cigarettes. It's been at least ten years since they smoked. Now, the man has a silver trailer in mind. He's thinking where he'll put it. Should he get a windmill? He's thinking about water, how he will dig and find it. How, in cupped hands, he will bring it to her. An offering, her lips grazing his palms while she drinks her fill.

The woman is beginning a novel. About a couple stuck on the moon on a rainy night in a Dodge diesel. They've run out of gas in her story. There's a dilemma; they don't have diesel on the moon. They order up love a la carte at the Heart's Desire Diner. A man comes across a river to deliver. He's carrying a jar filled with some kind of fluid that will move a mountain let alone a truck. An elixir. It's fiction, after all. Anything can happen. Anything will.

"Look," she says. And they do. The man and the woman are

looking through the windshield back toward the earth where they came from and it regards them, these familiar strangers, blue as a baby's eye, opening wide, wider.

Miniature Graceland

Why I'm still in Arkansas, a state I never thought I'd live in for love or money, I don't know. I came here for love but it didn't last. And money? Well, I get almost enough from disability to live on. The new four-lane went in right after my husband left and the old two-lane highway that goes through Winslow that was always jammed with trucks was suddenly deserted and quiet. I bought a peacock for the racket and to watch him spread his fan. I started making something in my yard to pass the time.

It started with an ordinary doll-sized house. Things just escalated from there: the meditation garden, the pond, the gold record museum, the concert hall. After a while I couldn't stop. Graceland grabbed hold of me and wouldn't let go until I had recreated all of it. It's not a public attraction; it's a private obsession and everybody stares at me when I go to the library. Well, let them look. Every village needs an eccentric, and around here, the competition is fierce. At least I don't harm anybody.

If I look back, there were signs. Literally. A bumper sticker on a Saab from California that was parked outside the Little Old Opry in West Fork said, "Who Died and Made You Elvis?" That made me think. I'm still thinking about it. And then I couldn't get the Paul Simon song out of my head that goes, "I'm going to Graceland, Graceland, Graceland, Tennessee." I began to see Elvis as a kid with all the toys he wanted, dabbling in the dreams of a man. God, on a kind of lonely trial run.

On the anniversary of his death, *60 Minutes* paid tribute, and showed him at his last concert. There he was, middle-aged, bursting out of a spangled jumpsuit, all those over-the-hill hands grabbing at him. He looked frightened by all that love he knew he couldn't live without. Graceland was the only place left to hide. At the peak of his career, I think even Graceland was too big a world for the King. Maybe he died in the bathroom because it was the smallest place he could find. I think of him as still looking for a small place he can fit inside. I know what it's like to be adored and tossed aside. So I built that small place for him.

What's strange is that Miniature Graceland would be picked on by the small. They were here last night, a ragged little army of children, pillaging, and I didn't even hear it happen. Now I pick up the splintered front door, place it carefully in the palm of my hand. I look for the wreath that went on it, no bigger than a quarter, and find it, crushed in the print of a size-twelve Reebok. So what if it's August? Santa's somewhere, jammed headfirst into the chimney. But it's the sight of the reindeer, all eight of them without legs, that does me in. There's no excuse to trash the place even if I do leave the Christmas decorations up all year long.

I've had it up to here. I am not about to be vanquished by the meanness in the kids who tore down what took me a whole year to build with my own two hands. Tonight, I prepare to meet the Vandals and the Huns.

I take a thermos of coffee and a load of buckshot and hide behind the bushes where I can get a good, clean shot. I wait.

I don't have to wait long. Here they come now, sniggering and slapping each other. There's the nerdy kid who works at the EZ Mart, the James Dean knockoff who has probably just graduated from letting air out of tires. And, to my surprise, the third is a kid I always thought of as being too sweet for his own good, who labored faithfully on his paper route on a pathetically rusted and squeaky bicycle rain or shine. He looks like the kind of kid who would cry in movies starring animals who stalwartly find their way home through a hundred miles of freeways and shopping malls after their family moved and left them behind.

James Dean swings his chain—it's a makeshift battleaxe

attached to a stick. It cuts the air, slices the dark like a hot knife through butter. A cruel whistle follows it around.

"Stupid bitch," he says. He laughs. "King, my ass, Cobain *rules.*" It sounds like an evil chant, and at the end of it the chain cracks into the roof, breaks it open as if it is no more substantial than a soufflé.

The nerd giggles, claps his hands over his mouth, and continues, doubled over. Sweet Kid doesn't move a muscle but stands there as if the chain's other end has been attached, in a metaphorical way, to his ankle all along. I could shoot them right now, but I'm mesmerized—there's something terrible and breathtaking about how what has taken so long to build up can so swiftly be brought down. It's like seeing the divine in action—all that giving and taking away. I feel I have seen something I shouldn't have, something God has known all along but keeps from us that will only make life harder rather than any degree more do-able if we see. But I can see it now: at the heart of violent destruction a certain shiver of beauty reigns.

The chain swings again, smacks across the half-buried mirror that makes the pond in the meditation garden. Shards fly up and the moon catches in some; they rain like silver needles on the ground. My peacock, Flannery, strides into view and stops. He opens his fan wide and the eyes tremble, staring from the intricate net of feathers. He shakes it and turns, but all that magnificence is wasted—they don't even look.

I aim into the air. I only want to scare them. But my hand is not steady; I can hardly hold the gun. My finger squeezes the trigger and a spray of buckshot rains against the wall. I've shot my own house. I have half a mind to keep shooting. I could get into this— tearing something down for the hell of it, watching it all fall down.

All but Sweet Kid run. "Cool," he says. He turns his head almost serenely toward the exact location of my hiding place. He turns and begins to walk away but he stops by Elvis's concert hall. He looks back at me to make sure I'm watching, then he gives it a little kick. Then another, harder. The wall caves in as if some armored tank has just burst through. Inside it, I'd put all the dolls I hated when I was a child, and they were legion. Predominantly Barbies, but a token Ken. I set them in tiny chairs to listen—twelve in all, like a sexy jury. I didn't bother with the outfits. In Miniature Graceland the girls face forward, naked and attentive and unashamed.

Sweet Kid stops. All those breasts and slim thighs and thickets of blonde hair, those aristocratic feet arched and ready for high heels and only a single Ken cowering among them. One Barbie Sweet Kid could have handled, picked it up, and laughed, but twelve is an army, an assault upon his fledgling redneck sensibilities, a phalanx of female flesh and identical take-no-prisoner smiles.

He doesn't run, though I know he wants to. He gives a pained little smile. Then he just slinks back into the kudzu.

In the morning, I'm on my knees again, peering through a hole in the roof. A bee floats upward out of the shattered house, a sign of something. A buzzing soul, maybe, just now resurrecting.

I begin to think seriously about revenge, maybe a hive of bees, hidden, that would teach these kids a lesson they would never forget. Trained bees who would come back when I called, swarm when I said.

The bee is a harbinger of more than revenge. It also might be a cure. After ten years' remission, I find myself at forty-nine years old at the mercy of an autoimmune disease I cannot predict let alone control whose symptoms: numbness, double vision, muscle weakness come with no warning, leave of their own accord. My husband, Arthur, a professor of English at the university, left me a year ago when my symptoms got worse again—he felt terrible, he said, but taking care of a potential invalid was not the life he'd ever imagined for himself and since he had a choice, he was going to take it, which meant a new job at Ole Miss. I was devastated, but if I had a choice, I would leave me, too. I didn't have a degree in anything except good looks, once, and those were on the way out, too. Boston born and bred, I was soon barely holding my own in the Ozarks.

Arthur left a lot of books behind and I read every single one of them. I felt a particular kinship with the writer Flannery O'Connor because of the disease we had in common. I even bought a peacock, her bird of choice, and named it after her. Every time it cries out in the night I can't help but think of her, her Christ-haunted South, the stories filled with recalcitrant children, deranged preachers, and one-legged women with advanced degrees. She *spoke* to me.

Flannery wrote and suffered in silence and died way too young. There wasn't much they could do back then. Now, there's a new medication, but it's distributed by lottery. My number didn't come up. It made me furious to have to gamble for my life. So I decided to take matters in hand, get my own medicine. I was on a mailing list for a national lupus support group and had read of a controversial therapy: bees, which they didn't recommend. Venom from the gradual accrual of administered stings over a year's time could force a production of antibodies that would destroy the disease, at least that was the theory. I picture a burning wind, a wildfire running through me while I go against every instinct to stand still and be stung, like a horse reasoning with itself to stay inside a burning barn.

I send for the bees—mail order like everything else. I don't want the post office knowing my business. The UPS man, Tate, whom I trust, brings them two days after I place the order with an apiary supply house. He comes up the sidewalk carrying a buzzing cardboard box punched with holes, lined with wire mesh screen.

"What in the world, Olivia?" he says, holding it at arm's length, turning his face, as if they might swarm out of there any second.

He's gotten used to a lot, coming here over the last year, watching me unpack a miniature pool table, a tiny chandelier, a dinette set in matching avocado green. But now his mouth drops open.

He hands me the box and when I take it from him my hand slides against his. My skin feels striped with heat where we touch. Why now, I wonder. I've hardly paid attention to him until this moment when he suddenly became a man to me. My legs may not be working but my hand is alive and well and pulsing. It's as if a secret panel just slid back from an inadvertent touch of a button, revealing a room inside of me that has always waited to be entered. But the secret room has a built-in alarm system and it goes off, right now. I can't look at him and wish I'd kept my hands to myself. Perhaps he's noticed I have no need for bees since I don't have a garden any more. I ask him to wait while I put the bees in the shed.

The box is alive. The bees seem to know they've arrived somewhere where they'll soon be let out. They're flying around, bumping against the cardboard gently—it almost sounds like it's raining in there. I tear off the packing slip and the taped instructions which say they have enough food for a week—five more days, counting the two they took to travel. I picture little box lunches filled with flowers, tiny thermoses of nectar. I shut the door and hope the cool dark settles them down until I can get up the nerve to let them loose.

"Little bastards," Tate says when I come back from the shed. He means the boys, not the bees. Now he's kneeling in the dirt, trying to see if he can fix the roof. I look down at him, his thin red hair managing to hold a frail glow from the sun. "It looks like London in the Blitz," he says. He looks genuinely undone by the damage the kids have done.

I think back to the first time he came here and remember he didn't fit the profile—that certain breed of deliverymen. He didn't gun the truck through the potholes like the cowboys who usually drove did, whooping as they left the ground, ruining the shocks and having a good time doing it. He drove at a sedate speed, with an Old World dignity, and his clipboard paperwork was impeccably filled out. And he found my place the first time—it's on an unmarked drive. Airborne Express gave up long ago. And the single word, "Graceland!" came hushed from his lips when he first saw what I'd made. He gave me an admiring look that caught me off guard. "Some people call it crazy, or stupid . . ." I began. He shook his head and interrupted. "It's absolutely wonderful!" he said.

"We have to do something," Tate says now. "I'll come by after my shift—maybe we can catch them." I look down at his brown, uniformed knees now gray in the dirt.

I notice there's a box behind him he must have set down when he first came. I try to remember what else I ordered besides bees. Then I do. I open it eagerly. Tate sits back on his heels, curious now, and when I have trouble getting through the packing tape he whips out a penknife and slits it open easily. We both carefully remove the bubble wrap. And there it is—the honeymoon suite—a heart-shaped bed with a red velvet cover. And best of all, there's a miniature lava lamp. Tate picks it up, upends it, watches the red globules ooze down. I pick up the red heart and hold it in my hand—it looks more like a box of dime-store Valentine chocolates than any kind of bed. I set it down between two white nightstands inside the roof-less house, in the room I prepared—gold lamé wallpaper, leopard rug. The heart is awfully red in there. Tate starts to put the lava lamp inside. He pauses. "Which side does Elvis sleep on?" he asks. "The left," I say, though it's a wild guess—it's just the side I would choose.

Now, I feel a sudden weakness, as if my muscles have turned liquid. But it's not a medical situation—it's spiritual. Or maybe it's a kind of free-range lust coming from left field because I'm glimps-ing something beneath Tate's brown-uniformed exterior—some-thing tender and accessible. But also, and I feel a lot of shame in this—I know for sure I'm losing ground—not only against the kids, but the lupus. Just this morning when I was brushing my hair, the brush fell from my hands after I realized I could no longer feel the wooden handle. I smacked my palm with the bristles. Nothing. It was something I saw, not felt. Soft and sharp became the same. I had lit a match with great difficulty and held it, watching the flame crawl down the wooden stem toward my fingers, and I watched, amazed, as the skin blistered, like it was somebody else's.

How much would have to burn before I could feel it? My mind had sense enough to blow the match out. The feeling came back a few minutes later, slowly, like the pins and needles in a leg that's been asleep trying to wake. It has been an unusually bad day.

Watching Tate now the thought comes over me that my entire body is falling asleep while my mind is helplessly awake, powerless to shut itself off. If I were kissed this minute could I still feel it? Would I know for sure if my lover came inside me?

There isn't time to think about all this now. There are the bees in the shed. There is this man kneeling beside me in my yard. There is this woman inside me, supple, sleek, sexual, fighting to get out. All I have to do is get up the nerve to let myself get stung a few hundred times.

The radio crackles from the truck. "Damn," Tate says. "How's half-past six. I'll bring Chinese."

"I've got a beer we can split," I say.

"I'll bring an extra, just in case."

He honks twice as the truck roars away.

I look into Elvis's bedroom—the sun shines straight down, right onto part of the heart. As I watch, a breeze comes up, one of those phantom things from out of nowhere, and blows some seeds down from a maple I'd planted. They whirl all over Graceland. Some come to rest in the bedroom, one nicks the edge of the bed and lands on the carpet. It looks like a shucked set of wings. The roof may be gone, but some of heaven has fallen in.

All kinds of ideas romp around in my head the rest of the afternoon, some welcome, some I wish I never thought: he genuinely likes me. Or, he thinks I'm a joke. He finds me entertaining but not particularly attractive. He and a pack of other UPS drivers have a secret quota of women customers, a tally of conquests at the end of the week. Or—there's something wrong with him. He's a highly functioning autistic savant or has terminal brain cancer with two months to live. Or, he's just an ordinary man with a healthy curiosity, and an open and imperfect heart.

I dump my entire top bureau drawer out on the bed and rummage through it, remembering what my mother said about the importance of underwear—how the elastic gave way on her briefs as she was walking by Marshall Fields in Chicago, how they pooled around her ankles, hobbling her, how she, as casually as possible, stepped out of them, picked them up and dropped them into her purse, snapped it shut, and went on. I always imagine the giddy freedom she must have felt walking down the busy street, naked underneath, the spring air caressing her, walking with a secret, sultry satisfaction inside her prim dotted Swiss dress. And now here I am with my sorry underwear—gray and stretched out. If any of these fell around my ankles I wouldn't bother to put them in my purse. I'd step out of them and gladly surrender them to the sidewalk for people to wonder how in the world they got there.

But here, at the bottom of the pile on the bed is a pink satin Chinese bag stitched with cranes and pagodas. Inside is a black lace bikini—a thong, really—something so clearly frivolous and sexy it can only be called lingerie.

I remember it was expensive, but I'd cut the tag off—that's how sure I was that I'd wear it. My husband left before I got the chance. Such extravagance and optimism—a few minutes of appreciative viewing before they'd be pulled passionately down my legs and flung to the far corner of some motel room for the maid to find in the morning. They'd only ended up in a sock drawer.

I pull off the stretched-out pair I have on and slip easily into the thong. I stand in front of the armoire mirror—I have a shape—and the black lace helps define it. I unhook my bra—my breasts do not completely sag, my nipples still work, harden instantly in the cool touch of air. I think of his hand, starting here, moving downward, my blood rushing to my skin to meet him, there. I would want me, if I were him.

I hardly recognize Tate when he arrives. He pulls up in a

Subaru that has seen better days. He wears a pair of blue jeans—ironed, I can tell by the sharp creases, and a T-shirt, also ironed, starched and tucked in. And a pair of those hiking sandals that make anyone's feet look like hooves. Maybe it was the uniform I found sexy, the clipboard, the charging steed of the indestructible truck. Now, he just looks civilian. Still, he's bringing me something, as always, only this time I don't have to sign for it. In one hand he's got a take out box of Chinese food, in the other, a bonsai tree in a shallow oval pot. He presents the tree to me. "Elvis needs some shade," he says.

I take the tree—it's perfect. It's so perfect I'm afraid to touch it, as if it will snap if I breathe too hard on its intricate branches. "It's beautiful," I say. "I'm touched. I really am." As soon as I say it I feel the truth of it, and the irony, too. I am touched, but I can't help but think of the phrase "touched in the head," which is what everybody around here thinks I am. I'm also losing my touch with lupus. I set the tree down quickly in Elvis's front yard.

"I just got the chow mein. Five Happiness. I didn't know what you'd like, but I figure that there's three or four out of the five that you might find suitable."

We sit on the park bench I'd ordered from Sears; it's sturdy enough for two. There's plenty of room for the both of us and the box in between.

I open the folded flaps and steam rises immediately, adding to the already humid air. He hands me a pair of chopsticks he had stuck in his back pocket like a comb.

I used to be really good at chopsticks, but these days I'm lucky if I can hold a pen long enough to get through a letter. I open the paper wrapper, take the two pointed ends and pull the golden sticks apart. But they don't break evenly. The top of one shears off, leaving the other with a large, splintered head.

"That's good luck," he says.

"Since when?"

He shrugs. "I just made it up."

"Well, since you're up on Chinese lore, what are the five happinesses?"

"Hmmmm," he says, and frowns as if he's searching deep within the dusty archives of arcane knowledge gathered over several lifetimes. "A home. Food." He lifts a swampy mess of noodles that dangles from his chopsticks.

"Those are the obvious ones," I say. "Maslov's hierarchy: survival, necessities. What about subtler desires?" I have managed to grip a shrimp firmly between the wooden tweezers and I get it all the way to my mouth without mishap. My skin feels flushed, tingling, but not like the forerunner of the old numbness coming on.

"Music," he says, with certainty. "Hank Williams. Poetry—Dylan Thomas, beyond the shadow of a doubt."

I consider these. He surprises me with the poetry. I would have guessed he'd pick the Razorbacks or fly-fishing.

"That's only four," I say, dropping a cashew in my lap.

"You pick the fifth," he says. "Ante up."

I don't have a snappy answer, though I search for one. I could say coffee ice cream but we've already covered food. I search for something subtle, a way to reveal myself without spilling my guts. I want to say "sex" but it's too naked. Too necessary. It makes me think of what scientists call Failure to Thrive, and I picture listless lab monkeys deprived of touch, how, given a choice, they would rather starve than not be held.

"The fifth happiness is faith," I say, which seems safe, like it could cover a lot of things, a way of saying hope without sounding too desperate. "I don't mean religion," I add quickly, suddenly worried he'll think I'm a Jesus Jumper. "I mean faith in the sense of believing absolutely in what you can't see."

He looks at me with unmistakable admiration. I feel a little flustered, and then I realize that the kind of faith I've been talking about includes faith in him to get the point, which I believe he has.

We finish the Five Happiness chow mein in a comfortable silence. I only find four things in there that could explain the name—beef, pork, chicken, shrimp. The fifth was not immediately apparent. Maybe the fifth happiness is by nature, a wild card, open-ended, yet to be defined.

We sit there, looking out over Graceland, which is a little shabby right now, though dusk helps.

"It looks nice—the tree," he says.

I murmur something illegible. But I hear this thought creeping in like a cold draft, like hitting one of those freezing currents while you're swimming in a warm lake. There is a tree now—*his* tree—in my Graceland. Mine. What if he starts bringing more things, stuffing it full of knick-knacks and Hummel statuary? What if he isn't interested in me at all but just wants a piece of Graceland? I feel like a mean kid forced to share and I want to shout, "Get your own!"

"We'll catch those kids—I just know it," he says.

I look at him, search his round face. It's not the face of a man with ulterior motives. Nor is it the face of a man with a growing desire. It's just a face, stretched here and there by smiles, contracted in places by unshed tears.

I reach over and put my hand on his. He doesn't flinch. He looks down, as if to verify that my hand is actually there. And slowly, gently, he lifts my hand from his, and places it on my lap. He pats it once, twice. I make myself sit still, though I imagine that the noise of my teeth grinding is unmistakably audible. I have an almost uncontrollable urge to slap him for not being brave enough.

Somewhere down the street, the volume on a stereo goes full on for about five seconds, then mysteriously falls silent. Pearl Jam or Smashing Pumpkins, probably. Both names suggest messiness, things squashed and oozing, like baby food.

"Nirvana," Tate sighs, but it is not a blissful sound.

The blood that was rising to meet his hand now makes a sharp turn, away from the heart, into the dark funnel of my mind. I can't stop now, something needs to take him down. "So," I say, "how did you become a UPS driver—I thought you had to be under forty or something."

He looks confused, but says quickly, "I passed the test—I do all right, I work out, I can lift heavy things. I passed the test," he says again.

The unsaid hangs in their air, a buzzard, waiting to move in. I deserve a retort—"Aren't you a little old for *this*?" meaning playing with doll houses, building a shrine for an overweight teenage king.

We sit there, miserably, turning our attention by necessity to the spectacle before us: the wrecked kingdom, the brave little tree.

We sit and sit and sit. The heavy air of evening settles over us.

"I meant to kiss you," I say.

Silence from him. Now I've really ruined it.

"Were you supposed to start, or was I?" he asks.

"I didn't get that far," I lied, knowing I'd already gone a lot further in my mind, all the way, to third base and then some. All the way home.

An armadillo waddles into the yard and Flannery flaps to his roost in the cedar tree. He issues a few mournful cries, then settles down for the night, surrendering to the din of cicadas.

"UPS drivers aren't pushovers," Tate says.

"I never thought so," I say.

"A lot of people think so," he says, turning toward me, agitated now. Even in this light I can see his flushed face glowing as red as his thinning hair. "They think we're out there like drones, servicing lonely housewives. I'm just doing my job. I'm just trying to be a decent person. I just came here to lend a hand."

Jesus, I think. Get a grip. Here it comes. He's going to back up the dumptruck of male woes, he's been hurt, he's looking for some woman to finally understand him. Now I'm going to hear about every lousy relationship, how he can't finish his novel, how he has vivid, unutterable memories of his childhood. I don't want to hear about it. I just wanted a kiss, for Chrissakes. A kiss dignified by honest desire, a little animal lust only slightly curtailed by human considerations. Two mouths pressing together in common misery and hope. A kiss!

Which I am not capable of giving or receiving right now. What I really want is everything connected to a kiss, where it might lead, out of the small dark crawlspace of fear into a wide-open, sun-washed field.

He gives his hand over, a consolation prize, I suppose, but he took too long. I don't want it. I take it anyway. A hand. Five fingers. Impeccable nails. No rings, not even pale places where they once had been.

Tate leaves, with no more talk of helping me catch the kids. I think we were both relieved to have the evening end. My thoughts race around like little things in a maze, too scared to make sense of the way out. How had I gotten so cynical? When did I subscribe to the theory that men would always thwart me any way they could, hoarding their kisses or confidences or even just clear directions, fair estimates and honest labor—whatever it was that I needed from them?

I walk unsteadily into the yard. The world has turned away from Orion, which had earlier been overhead—scientific logic tells me this is the explanation, but to me it seems Orion is striding away, that it's me that's standing still. How did I get so angry? I can't blame this on lupus entirely, but surely it's hindering my ability to think clearly. I would leave too—I'd slink off in my Subaru if I had one. I'm becoming a woman expecting the worst. A royal pain in the ass. A shrew. I could join the mean kids, become their crazy leader, terrorize the neighborhood with vindictive glee.

It's time to stop this. Now. While I still can.

The bees stir in their box as I close the door. The place used to be a potting shed, back when flowers still commanded my attention. The place is full of stacked, chipped clay pots, some still holding the remains of chrysanthemums killed by a hard freeze early last fall. I light a couple of votive candles I've always kept in here with a book of matches. I used to sneak out here and smoke cigarettes after my husband and I quit. I pull the chrysanthemum out by its roots—it comes easily—and the leaves crackle when I squeeze them in my hand. I know that bees hate smoke—that's the way you get them out of their hives when you want their honey.

I light the weed and it flares suddenly, the skeleton of the plant black, curling inside the orange flame. I smack it on the dirt floor to put it out—sparks fly and dissolve in midair and a voluptuous plume of smoke pours forth like a potion from a witch's cup. I open the jar I brought with me. I smear myself with honey.

The bees pelt the inside of the box, desperate to get out. I stand there and listen for a while. As a child, they were always my worst fear, more terrifying than anything that crawled. I would swat wildly at them and run—they seemed aimed, on a mission to get me. And now my life has come to this: I have summoned my demons, and they wait for my command.

It should be easy to open the box, but the knife keeps slipping from my hands, from weakness or fear, I can't tell which. I wish I had Pandora's naieveté. Unlike her, I know what's in there waiting to get out. But I also know in advance what she didn't learn until later. Mixed in with all the spites and pestilence at the bottom of the barrel is hope.

The article said you start slowly. One sting, then gradually work your way up to twenty stings three times a week. I don't have time for that. I want it all at once. This may kill me. The thought comes like the moth that is now fluttering in and out of the candle flame. What *is* light? Can't it tell the difference between the kind that will lure and destroy it and the kind that will let it be near? It loves the light, it has to have it, no matter what; it's not an option. And what is it that I have to have? I try to imagine a man for myself who would appreciate the question. A man who would love me no matter what I lost—my sight, my legs, my mind. But maybe a lover's touch is too easy. What I *require* is tantamount to a gesture from the hand of God—the capacity to be *moved*.

For two seconds, I am an eager child, lifting the lid of possibility, peering into paradise, then all hell breaks loose, only in slow motion. The bees drift upward as if drugged. They don't even notice me. Confused, they career, ricochet slowly off the walls of the shed. They're too stoned to sting me—I'm the least of their worries, I hardly stack up as a threat. I move through the buzzing cloud and they only make their way around me. I become their tree. They land. Then they find the honey.

The first sting hurts—it's on the palm of my hand. I yelp like a stepped-on puppy. I've forgotten how much stings hurt. I cover my face with my hands and make myself stand still.

My arms, my legs, are covered; I am a woman in a gown of bees, a queen penetrated by an entire hive. They keep right on stinging, not all of them, but enough. Silence comes down over me like a bell jar descending. Inside it, my body hums and hurts. The bees are a part of me now, they move with me, they breathe as I do, when I do; there is nothing between us now.

A noise from above—a cry rending the smoky air. A sound of wings through the buzz of locusts. I think it might be the angel of death, but it's only Flannery making a ruckus. And then I hear the chain, the terrible chain, cracking against wood.

I move toward the door and the bees come with me. When I open the door and step into the yard, the bees do not leave but start zinging around me like electrons around a nucleus—we make a universe, the bees and I; we cross the threshold back into the world.

They turn—the two boys swinging chains; Sweet Kid stays his ground. Mouths drop open; chains fall to the ground. The two come to their senses and run; Sweet Kid stands his ground, frozen to the spot.

The bees, drunk on air now, slowly leave me. I feel as if I've lost my skin. I hear Sweet Kid cry out. I begin to swell, expand, my body soft and rising even as I sink to the ground. I smell smoke, but it's not coming from the shed. I turn. It's the bonsai, encased in flames, each perfect branch limned in fire.

There's only Sweet Kid gasping as if his heart will burst, something in him constructing a logic of cause and effect, feeling somehow responsible for everything.

Sweet Kid stops crying, his terror displaced by awe. His face looms but keeps its distance; he looks huge from the ground. He smells strongly of the urine he wet himself with. I watch it happen, the change come over him, the healthy fear giving way to a cool superiority as it dawns on him that without my bees, I have no power. I can see him hating the helplessness before him. I swear I can feel the idea of dominion occur to him.

I hear a car, and so does he. We both watch it roll forward, without headlights. The engine is off—there is only the sound of its heavy weight on gravel, advancing.

The Subaru, slinking back. The door opens. Something luminous, white emerges. It doesn't look like Tate at all. Black hair, I can tell from here. He's carrying something shiny, some implement that glints in the moonlight, but I can't make it out.

When he steps into full view, Sweet Kid gasps but stays rooted to the spot. I can hardly believe my eyes—maybe bee venom is a hallucinogen—some great drug we somehow missed in the sixties. It's *him*. The King. He never really left; he's here again. in a white-spangled jumpsuit holding a National steel guitar.

He's dazzling, his pompadour a sleek plumage that would make Flannery envious, but I catch a glimpse of the bird on the roof, tail tucked and the golden eyes concealed. Sweet Kid comes to his senses and bolts. I stay put and stare.

I know that it's really Tate in a rented costume, but still. For a minute it's Elvis Aaron Presley in Graceland, come to lend a hand. He doesn't have to sing. He doesn't have to do anything but stand there. He takes my breath away.

Should I call out to him? I don't think I will. I don't want to be taken in hand, rushed to some emergency room, pumped full of antihistamines to block the venom. I've come this far; I want it in every part of me. I'm not going to die, I can tell, it's just that everything will change. It isn't what I thought I wanted, or what I asked for, but at this moment, struggling to rise to my knees in Graceland, I am ready to receive.

I have never felt so porous, so full of light. My blood has turned to clear nectar in my veins and it runs through me like a song. I turn my head toward Graceland, and from this perspective, I am its god, a moon face looking through a window. Any second now I will become small enough; I will be let in.

He raises a hand in the silvery air. He sees me. Elvis Aaron Presley, having successfully defended my kingdom, gets in his Subaru and drives away. Left on Lonely Avenue, right on Main.

Snake Woman

Lila just got written up: "Snake Woman of the West," the *Chicago Tribune* called her. Now what does that make me? In the photograph of us along with the article, Lila looms in the foreground, all six feet of her, holding out a five-foot rattler by the tail. Her Stetson shades her face so that it looks like a phase of the moon; her eyes are in the dark of it, her mouth in full sun, her jaw set as if she is trying hard to keep her teeth together. Mean, but looking good. And there I am in my wheelchair, squinting into the sun because the photographer wouldn't let me wear my hat. "The derby doesn't make it," he said, "doesn't look Western enough." Which was the point. Which was lost on him. I put it on just to piss him off. He drove down here in a rented minivan, looked like he'd stopped in San Antonio long enough to hit the gift shops and get a $700 pair of Luchesse hand-made boots. He pointed one of those pointy toes at Lila for approval. "That's lizard," she said. "Not snakeskin. You've been had."

The picture sets in a frame in the kitchen now where Lila can get a good look at herself every day. She's proud of being called the Snakewoman, says it suits her more than her own name. She places a lot of importance on names—is proud of her birthplace, Sanderson, Texas, because it's the banded king snake capital of the world.

My given name is Alexander, which Lila says will take a lot of living up to; I told her that's why I changed it to Chance, which can mean just about anything.

Personally, I have a lot of respect for snakes and sometimes lately I think Lila has gone too far. The first one she shot in the back yard after an argument—probably when she first got a good whiff of hundred proof on me. Truth is, I'm a drunk—was, am, will be; she's just not ready to accept it. She slammed out the kitchen door and then turned right around and came back in. I thought she'd come back to apologize, but she grabbed her shotgun and went out again. I heard only one shot and there she was, bringing the bastard in the kitchen still twitching and writhing, then it stopped and hung down straight and stupid as a rope.

"I'm going to skin this thing and make a necktie out of it—it'll suit you perfectly." She thrust it at me. "Here's lookin' at you, Chance. Go ahead, drink up." She had an expression on her face I'd never seen before, but have seen many times since: satisfied and inflamed with righteousness, as only a person who's gotten the last word can be. I remember feeling sorry for the snake.

Lila wheeled me out of the VA hospital in San Antonio one day after two months of visiting her daddy, which turned out to be a total waste of time. He shared a room with me—cirrhosis of the liver—and would talk half the night about his glory days singing with a band on the honky-tonk circuit, basically all the places off highway 90 between San Antone and Van Horn. Lloyd Stanley, the Singing Cowboy. He was having himself a time, he said, until Lila slammed him into rehab. He said he would start drinking again the minute he got out just to spite her and that he'd never forgive her as long as he lived, which didn't turn out to be a very long time. You'd think it was his wife he was talking about, not his daughter. It was like he'd taken a vow to bust her chops, and he was true right to the end.

When she came to see him, he wouldn't say a word to her, just stared at her through the whole visiting hour until she left. She'd stare right back—I've never seen such a stubborn woman. She'd go ahead and ask him questions anyway, and he wouldn't even grunt an answer. Finally, one day I couldn't stand it any longer and when she asked him, "Can I do anything for you?" I found myself answering, "You can come over here. You can waste your breath on someone who'll appreciate it." To my total surprise she got right up and came over to my bed. She sat on the edge of it. Her eyes were a disturbing shade of green, and she turned them full on me. I swear she didn't blink for nearly five minutes. She didn't say anything, but I could feel her thinking. "Well?" she seemed to say. "Well?" "Viridian," I blurted out. She said, "What?" and I had to clear my throat and say it all over again. "It's what color your eyes are." It was a wild guess—something I saw on a paint tube in the art therapy room and sounded exotic enough to be right. "Is that an actual color?" she asked. I nodded and she went right on to the next question: "How'd you lose your leg—in the war?" "In a manner of speaking," I said. "It was my own war and I lost it. I'm only here 'cause I did a tour in Nam—not even wounded." Of course I didn't tell her the whole truth, and she didn't ask, maybe she took one look at me and knew I was a long way from "coming to believe."

We talked every day for two weeks. I couldn't tell if she was doing it to spite her daddy or if she genuinely liked to talk to me. She told me about the time in high school she was rodeo queen in Pecos, and I made up a story about my mama being a fortuneteller. In truth, the only future she foresaw was mine. "You're going to hell in a hand basket," she'd say, "if you don't get yourself straightened out." Little did she know I'd end up so literally crooked. In any event, Lila's daddy slipped into a coma and it didn't matter one way or the other what he thought any more, but he warned me that first night after Lila let me look at her that I shouldn't trust her as far as I could piss. What a thing to say, what a way to measure how much faith you've got left in your only child.

She got me out of there as soon as I was fitted with a prosthetic. I don't recall a discussion about it—she just said she was bringing me home. Took me to her ranch outside Sanderson, which was the real deal: a dog, a few cattle well fed, a horse, a windmill. A backdrop of ragged mountains. The Southern Union Pacific tracks stitching along the edge of it. The minute I got there I took off the leg and put it under the bed. It was about as pink as a shrimp and twice as ugly. I didn't like lurching around with it—in the chair I felt more like a man. I didn't know how to act or what she wanted from me. I tried to do little things around the house for her—I've always been good with my hands. One day when I was sanding a chair that I'd stripped to refinish, she stood over me, watching me work. The back of my neck was burning as she stared at me with those viridian eyes of hers, and the next thing I know she was kneeling down on the floor, closing her eyes as she took my fingers in her mouth one at a time, sucked on them as if they were honey-sweet rather than the varnish they must have tasted of. And she conjured up a likewise hunger in me and I found myself doing something I'd never even thought of before: I licked her entire body with the tip of my tongue—there was no place on her I didn't go. And then, oh, how we rolled around all afternoon on that blue shag rug, a little square of heaven come down to earth in west Texas hell.

It didn't take all that long to lose the fire. She got pissed at me for refusing to wear the leg, and in that way, I guess I was as stubborn as her daddy. It was like the old man's pathetic spirit sneaked into me before he died so I could haunt Lila for him—the bastard was just not going to let her rest. Before I knew it, I started drinking again. I could say the devil made me do it, but I swear it was Lloyd Stanley, and the first night I got knee-walking drunk, which is hard to do with one leg, I knew it was only a matter of time before she would throw me out.

That's when the snake thing started to become like a religion for Lila. After she nailed all the snakes in the yard she started hunting on the rest of her four hundred eighty acres. At first it was kind of amusing—off she'd go with a rifle and heavy boots at sundown, a knapsack to tote 'em back in. She began to do it every night, like she couldn't rest until she'd cleaned out the county. She never got bit—she bragged about that. I started laying bets that she eventually would, and I tried to get her take to an anti-venom kit with her just in case. But she preferred to think she had a charm that kept her safe—a tinny-looking wagon wheel the size of an old silver dollar. It had the letters of her name stamped on it. Her father had given it to her when she was twelve years old, got it from an amusement park in Corpus he was passing through after he left her mom. She said the reason it was lucky was that he'd spelled her name wrong—Lilla. The extra L, she said, stood for luck. How like her to turn something hurtful into a sign of grace. But to me it was just another sign of a father not having any idea who his daughter was, a thing to remind her every day of her life that everything about her, down to her name, was wrong.

Fathers are experts at that—you can't shut them up, even when they're in the ground. The first time my old man took me deer hunting and I missed what he considered an easy shot he called me a useless piece of shit. Useless. I heard that word so many times it was what I began to answer to. I thought if I came home from Nam with a medal that might vindicate me. I didn't get a medal, but I came home one-legged, with a lie about how it happened, which didn't shut him up, just lowered the volume.

Anyway, Lila wasted no part of the snakes. She fed the meat to the dog and even sneaked some in a stew for us once, but I bit down hard on one of those tiny vertebrae and knew it was nothing that came from a chicken. I took it out of my mouth and set it on her bread plate—sounded thin as a dropped dime. She picked it up. I thought she'd say she was sorry—I might have choked on it. "Earrings," is what she said, studying it, already planning on how to get the hooks attached.

She made everything out of snakeskin—scabbards and belts and hatbands. There was a logic to these items. People paid big money for such things. She showed them to me once in *Esquire* magazine—a big square-jawed bastard with wet hair and a suit on with no shirt underneath, his hands on his hips, parting the jacket just enough to show off the belt. The caption beneath him said, "Accessory to die for—Rattlesnake Belt, $300." You couldn't pay me three hundred dollars to wear one of those.

Pretty soon Lila was buying kits to make clocks, cutting out little circles of skin to paste where the hours were. Then it was pieces stuck on lighters and tape measures and nail files and any goddamn thing that had a surface that would take glue. "What are we going to do with all this?" I asked, wild-eyed when she brought in a Sony Walkman—mine!—with a snakeskin slipcover.

"You can run the gift shop," she said. "You're wasting away out here, Chance. You got to get a life, and since you won't, I'm going to give you one." Then she slammed the screen door behind her as she set out for the evening hunt.

Hell, yes, I was pissed! Just because she was feeding me and loving me every once in a while (which took less and less time lately) didn't mean she got to assign chores like I was some kind of hired hand. I brought in some money—my disability checks covered the bills. And now here's my Lila, my beautiful green-eyed Lila, armed to the teeth, an Amazon with a lot of hard miles on her, a woman with a mission, which is not just snakes any more, but me. A gift shop! Twenty miles of bad washboard, flash-flooded open-range road—who does she think will find us? "I'll take an ad out in Fort Stockton," I said. "Don't you dare," she said. "Whoever finds us will feel they've discovered us all on their own. We'll be a well-kept secret."

"Like you discovered me," I asked, then wondered, if I was her secret, how well kept I was.

"I didn't discover you, I found you—there's a difference." She left me sitting there, her words like a wind stirring up the dust. Found. Like something shiny picked up from the floor, examined, found worthless, thrown down again.

The days get purposeful, tiresome. I grow to hate the sound of the Singer; it's the sound of my fate being hemmed up. I can't stand the thought of Lila's fingers on that skin, feeding it so patiently beneath the foot, the way the silver needle looks, when she makes it go slow, like it's drilling between her fingers.

I start driving—it's come to this. I put the leg on so I can work the clutch, but take it off as soon as I get in the door at home. On my first trip I drive all day and wind up at the dump outside Del Rio. Some of my best memories are the ones with my grandfather at the dump in McAlester, Oklahoma, on Saturday mornings, picking through all the crap other people had no use for. My grandfather cleaned it up and sold it at weekly yard sales. I made change for him and felt proud to be trusted with money, to be counted on to get it right.

The first thing I find today is a bronze baby shoe, the left one. Who would throw such a thing away? I put it in my pocket. In no time I fill up both. A grenade, of all things, harmless, unpinned. An egg beater, a saw blade. I get a box. I have no idea what I'm going to do with it all, but I found these things and somehow I feel responsible to them now.

When I get home I dump the stuff on the ground. I pick up the baby's shoe. It weighs a lot for such a little thing and then I think—why not put it on display? Screw the gift shop, I'm going to make a museum! So I tie a string to the shoe—there's a ball of twine I found—and the next thing you know I'm tying it to an old hitching post. It dangles, spins in the breeze. Then I hang the grenade next to it just because it's what I grab next, unintentional, but like most amazing unrelated things, there's a weird kind of sense to the two being next to each other. The wind shifts and pushes them together, not too hard. They almost chime.

I can't get the rest of the stuff up fast enough, and in half an hour it's all banging around, clunking and tinking in the wind.

"Look," I say to Lila, who's woken from her nap and heading out for the evening hunt.

She stops, actually stops. Even though she's well on her way, she cocks her head. She looks. And then she does something else. A slow smile slides across her face. Lila listens.

Lila would be the last to admit she's afraid of anything. She's certainly not afraid of snakes, but that's an unnatural kind of fearlessness, fueled by the fact she's got something to prove. Her daddy did a lot more than spell her name wrong on a cheap medallion—he tried to defeat her every day of her life. She has plenty of stories of how she'd drive him to all those honky-tonks, hang around until he fell off the stage, then pour him into the car and drive him home. She told me he was a genius of a liar. He professed to be sticking to a two-drink limit, but rigged up the washer fluid container under the hood, filled it with vodka, and ran the line through the dashboard and straight into a carton of orange juice he'd top off every time they pulled in for gas and he'd send her to pay. "That sonofabitch," Lila said, "was sittin' there gettin' loaded, thanking his higher power for showing him the alternate route to heaven." Things went from bad to worse until one day, after not seeing him for two weeks because she went to the rodeo in Pecos, she came home to find him on the couch in his boxer shorts, his bottles and the ashtray and the bedpan and the remote for the TV all within easy reach. That's when she put him in the hospital. All the way there he insisted he could stop drinking anytime. "If you can stop drinking for half an hour I'll buy you a hat." The ultimate Texas challenge. Well, he didn't get a hat, and she didn't save his life. Out of all that, she ended up with me, more of the same.

You want to see Lila scared? Want to see Lila cry? Just turn up the volume on Patsy Cline. I did last night before I knew what it did to her, that it was Lloyd's favorite music and he'd play it loud whenever he'd go on a bender. Lila screamed at me to shut it the fuck off, and I waved her away. "Crazy" was and is my all-time favorite song in the world and I damn well was going to hear it all the way through at a volume through which it could be properly appreciated. But she went out the back door to the breaker box and just shut the whole house off with a yank of the switch. I sat there in the dark, mad as hell. Then I heard a strange sound—a moaning, like the dog had been shot. I crawled through the living room on my hands, not bothering with the chair, and got myself into the yard. It was the dog moaning, but it wasn't shot. There was Lila down on the ground, punching the poor bastard, and the dog, beside itself with two different needs, cowering from the blows and trying to lick her face at the same time.

We all ended up in a heap, Lila shaking, then sobbing like her heart was breaking, which it surely was. An old break, I guess, like the way a bone heals when it was never set right—a weakness in the structure. And as I held her out there in the dirt of the yard, I knew her heart wouldn't open up to me. It made sense to me then, why we were together. The wounded always find each other; sooner or later pain surely clings to pain.

It was not so far a stretch to go from there to making love. You get inside a woman and you think you've finally gotten somewhere but it just brings you close enough to feel the fence, to know there's no way to get there from here.

Lila wouldn't even look at me—during or after. It was as if I'd already seen too much, but she was the one who turned away. I clung to her to keep her there just a little longer. I felt a space beneath us as if the earth itself were heaving open. I thought about the fact that we were stupid to be lying on the ground—the snakes were out that time of the evening. But it wasn't the snakes that were the danger right then. It was love, what it wanted of you, the fear that when it finally comes to you it might not be able to find a big enough place to breathe.

We lay there in the dirt looking up at the sky, at separate stars. It seemed only the scattershot ones were overhead right then, not the ones that added up to something, but the extras, not needed for dippers, bears, and kings.

The days are shorter now; water runs cool in the pipes. These are the things you measure the turn of a season by, never mind the calendar. Lila has been going out every evening, determined to get as many snakes as she can before they go under ground for the winter. The gift shop is stuffed with useless crap. The great hordes come—maybe one or two people a week. And my museum, which began as a kind of fence for the parking lot, has spilled across the road like it has a mind of its own and is heading on out of here, showing me the way. Yesterday I found a pair of crutches and hung those up. I also found a slew of old knives. It's an odd accumulation blowing around, hardly anybody to see or hear it except Lila and me. She says she likes it, that it's a wild noise, that I've given the wind a voice. But days like this, when the wind is strong and she's in the house sleeping, I wheel myself up and down the rows and it sounds to me like music coming from a strange world I should know better than to set foot in and I can only think that now the wind, too, wants something from me.

Today, I've brought the final thing to hang in the museum— my fake leg. I put it next to the baby shoe and the grenade.

When I finish hanging it I sit back to admire the juxtaposition. I've got a bottle of single-malt scotch I've been saving, hid inside a broke guitar. I drink quite a bit though I came for just a taste. I had meant to make it last. I do more thinking than is good for me and I want more than I can hope in this world to have: my leg back, my woman sweet on me again, for my mama to tell my future one more time; surely my life won't completely turn on me.

Nobody hardly comes to the museum. Most days I put the Honest John box out with a stack of paper sacks and at the end of the day I wheel out there to collect—once there was a check from a German bank with a number I couldn't read written in. Most times there's less than a dollar and a half.

Today, I watch a puff of dust on the horizon that can only mean a car coming. Who can this be on a Tuesday afternoon? If anybody shows up, it's usually on the weekend. An old blue Cadillac slowly comes into view—it just seems slow, actually, because when it comes closer I can see the thing bucking through the potholes, a great wall of churned dust behind. It roars past, then screeches to a halt. I hear it clunk into reverse, then it backs up, fishtailing, until it's even with me. The motor shuts down, but takes a long time to stop dieseling. A man the size of Orson Welles in his later years heaves himself out. He squints at me but doesn't say anything. He's got a bolo tie on with the biggest scorpion in amber I've ever seen. He fishes in his pocket for something, then takes out a roll of Butterscotch LifeSavers. He peels back the paper, enough to get four of them out at once—the rind of paper flaps in the wind. He pops them in his mouth, then looks around. "What the hell is all this?" he finally asks after a long time of trying to figure it out.

"Museum," I say. "Wonders of the World."

"Is it for sale?" He peels back another mess of LifeSavers—finishes the roll.

"For sale?"

"How much?" he asks.

"It's not," I say.

He shrugs. Studies it some more. "What's it for?"

"I like looking at it."

He studies me. He nods toward the gift shop, then looks back down the road, wide and empty as a runway. "Busy this time of year, Christmas and all."

"What do you want?" I ask, gripping the wheels of my chair hard, rearing it up a little, which must look about as ridiculous as a cat puffing up in front of a Saint Bernard.

"I want to meet the Snake Woman," he says. "I come to meet her, not you."

"She's not here," I lie.

"You her trainer, her keeper?" He stares pointedly at my empty pants leg flapping in the wind. "You get bit, or what?"

I wish I had Lila's gun. I'm just drunk enough to use it. I'd put him and his car and his bolo tie in the museum, bronzed.

I hear the screen door slam and my heart drops. It's Lila, and she's coming right this way.

She's got her rifle, ready to hunt. She walks over to us, sizes up the man. She's at least as tall as him, and suddenly I wish I had my leg so I wouldn't be down here at knee level.

"You the one that called yesterday?" she asks him.

"Roy G. Hurley. Yes, ma'am, the same."

"Hang on a minute, I'll be right back."

She ducks inside the gift shop. For one crazy minute I'm sure she's packed her bags and that she's riding off with this guy, that I've finally driven her mad and she's got no choice except to leave me sitting here in this trash heap I've made. I feel the old panic swell up—I can't breathe, I sweat like a pig, I hardly know where I am. It's all I can do to turn my head, to look at her as she's coming out the door. She's got a bottle in her hand, full of milky liquid.

Roy Hurley looks at me and laughs as he takes the bottle from her. He hands her two fifty-dollar bills. He turns to Lila again. "How do you milk 'em?"

"It's a little tricky, but not particularly hard—you get a jar and clamp 'em onto it so their jaws are spread—they just shoot it right in there."

"Snakespit—god damn," he says, shaking his head. He holds up the bottle, shakes it a little. Then he climbs slowly back in his car, packing himself in behind the steering wheel. He thanks Lila, completely ignores me. He starts up the car and a great blue cloud of smoke spews from the pipe. He leans out the window. "You decide to sell, you let me know. Folk art—it's all the rage."

Lila looks out over the museum, and I watch her do a slow double-take on the leg twirling there next to the grenade and the baby shoe. "You got a mean sense of humor, sweetheart. Even so, I'm starting to feel real sorry for you."

Last-word Lila turns on her heel and goes, leaving me with my leg twirling on a line. I still can hardly breathe. And the white rat that lives inside my head nibbles on a little more of my nerves. I can't get it out of my head—Lila's face when she first got a close look at the stump, just after love, the look of a woman taken aback and trying not to show it and then that other, final look of heart-broke resignation: the look of a beautiful woman once again set-tling for less.

Night comes on fast—too fast, the dark a thing with boots on, walking right this way. It throws its shadow around like a man you owe money to and can't ever hope to pay.

Lila's been hunting farther and farther away, not coming home until dawn; the snakes are few and far between. The bed is a lonely place, and I take my pleasure whatever way I can, but it's about as satisfying as milking a cow. Tonight, the worst part is I actually cry when it's over. The house is empty and listening to a man in pain; I imagine it's not sympathetic. I think I hear a sound outside the window. It can only be Lloyd Stanley, peering through the glass, laughing at what has wound up in his daughter's bed.

Right then Lila comes in the back door—she's early. Cupboards bang, drawers screech and shut. She must have found the scotch in the sack of beans. I hear the glass filling, the squeak of a chair as she settles into it. Lila never drinks. I'm about to go in there to see what's wrong when I see her move like a thing through water, a dreamy sway slowly filling the bedroom doorway. Silence buzzes in the room. I don't know what she wants—she hasn't wanted anything in such a long time.

"Alexander?" she whispers.

I don't know how to answer. My heart's stalling out in my chest and the thought finally comes clear to me that's been months arriving: I am afraid of her now. I've made myself a slow-moving target. She could turn her snake gun on me and finish the job. There's a part of me that might be grateful. She was the one listening outside the window—I'm sure of it—which makes her the only person in the world that's ever heard me cry. Women think they want a man's tears until they actually see them, then they have to rearrange his face, take it down from high plains drifter to lonely, shriveled child.

"Alexander," she says, a little louder. She waits.

She sighs. It's a sad sound, not a mean one. The stinging scent of burnt gunpowder drifts off her like a dangerous perfume. Her boots creak as she turns. I could stop her with a word, but right now I can't even say her name.

From the window I see the spike of light from her flashlight as she makes her way toward the rocky hills. I haul myself into my chair and roll down the porch ramp she built the day I got here, wheel down the rows of the museum and cut my leg off the line. It falls with a thud on the ground, looks like a doll part, magnified and strange.

I can still see the flashlight. She's moving slow, searching now, and I've maybe got a chance of catching up. All I know is I have to follow her. The moon is going down, dropping fast. The dark crawls across the *bahada,* chasing the last edge of moonlight. A mile-long train wails across the valley, its three lights blazing.

I follow her, jerky as a puppet at first, then finally I get the hang of it, but the ground is rough and it's slow going. At least she's not stalking straight out and purposeful like she usually does; Lila's wandering tonight.

How much can you know about a woman in less than a year except to feel the emptiness in any room she leaves? Is it enough time to know that she can keep a secret if you give her one, or that she'd risk her own life for yours if there came a time? Can you say you'd do the same? Whatever love we'd once put into each other had run down the drain. I gave her my need—the only thing about myself that I knew would last forever. And what had she done about it except set it aside as if it did nothing but call up her own?

I follow her up a long hill and when she disappears between some boulders I think that this is a picture of how it will be when she's gone forever—me stumbling after her, a disappearing trail of light where she's last been.

"Lila!" I call, needing to hear her voice coming back. Is she hiding now, keeping quiet, laughing to see how I'm trying to come to her?

When I finally clear the rise I see her light—it's not moving, but lying on the ground, fanning through scrub and rock. Lila's crouched upon the ground like a creature about to leap.

The light catches what's just beyond her: a section of coil thick as my arm. I know by the color it's a diamondback. A fierce buzz emanates from its tail. Lila doesn't move. She and the snake stare at each other two feet apart—easy striking distance.

"Don't move," I whisper, but of course she knows that. Still, I can't believe it—she's inching forward on her hands and knees and the snake only draws its head back a little as if it's having second thoughts about what to do, as if it's curious more than anything. She inches even closer and the snake holds its ground. They can't be more than a foot apart.

There it is, the face she's hunted all along, shot from a distance, now as close as a kiss. She's daring it to strike her. Or is it playing with her, taunting her closer? For a moment, I actually believe Lila has managed to hypnotize the snake, that maybe all along she's been working up to this—to take it up in her bare hands.

Lila's mouth is moving. I can't hear words, but I know. She's singing. It's not exactly pretty—it's more like eerie crying or a high-pitched prayer. There's a spirit moving on her, into her, and the snake is surely listening.

One step is all it takes—there's only inches between one life and the next. The snake whips its head around as I lurch forward. The entire body shoots toward me like a loaded spring. It strikes once, twice, and keeps on going at the plastic leg, determined to break through. I don't feel it, but I imagine I can—two points of heat drilling into me, the venom like a stream of lava racing through the blood, aimed straight for the heart. The snake beats itself against the stubborn leg, emptying its venom, wasting its best asset on something it can't even begin to hurt.

The snake stops, finally, and slides into the rocks as if it has had enough and can hardly wait to get beneath the ground. Lila isn't singing now. Lila isn't doing anything. She doesn't appear to be in her body at all. Then she starts shuddering—all the adrenalin escaping and running wild now through her veins.

I get down on the ground. I don't know whether she'll let me near her. What a time to want a woman, when she's got a look on her face like I've taken something meant for her or have given her something it might cost her plenty to keep. I just watch her, from about the same distance the snake had been. I see what it saw—a round, plain face, frightened, eyes more a depthless black now than any kind of green. Her mouth is still open, sung out. I take the look she gives me—a nakedness, a soul coming loose, within reach. I hold out my hand and it shakes—there's only one of two ways this thing can go. I could come to harm; I could come to mystery.

The Angel of Vermont Street

For as long as she lives and probably longer Alice will never forget the face of the man she killed last summer. She was thinking of his face again, as she did whenever she sat still long enough. And if memory truly lasted beyond earthly life, then she knew he had taken something of her with him when he closed his eyes and died—the memory of her face—an angel that had at long last shown herself and come to gather him home. She wondered for the hundredth time if he even knew she was the one who hit him.

The bicycle—it had fallen on its side, one wheel crumpled— no more substantial than a child's pinwheel beneath the car, the other wheel still spinning crazily as if it only wanted to free itself from the frame and roll safely away. He had made no sound as she leaned over him. But his eyes were luminous, clear. When she moved her head so that the street light directly above them cast its full illumination, his pupils failed to respond, leaving him wide open to the reach of light and the shape of her moving slowly above him. When he closed his eyes she moved her head again. Her shadow passed across his face like the shadow of earth shielding the moon from the full force of the sun.

She had learned later that he was partially crippled to begin with, that the bicycle moved him through the world, that his hands held the handlebars only by some sheer miracle of faith. The newspaper had said, quoting someone who knew him from the men's shelter where he lived, "He was an accident waiting to happen." But he had happened to her, come out of nowhere on a curve on Vermont Street. He'd lost his balance, surely, slid in the rain. She had not—she was almost certain of this—run into him. He had run into her, or at least fallen precisely in her path. Had he planned it? Was this a botched attempt at collecting disability benefits, a claim to live on for the rest of his life? Or had he meant to go further—all the way beneath the wheels?

His body. Breaking. That was what she heard. Solid and heavy against the thin steel of her foreign car. The twisting of the bicycle frame. A sound she still hears repeatedly. There was no scream, no cry, just the body taking it, that final meeting with a faster thing.

She had just come from John's house. A coworker, though he was with the Border Patrol in the field. She had told him she couldn't do what he was asking of her anymore. Isn't that the way it had gone? Wasn't he the one who had gone too far one night, his hands on her neck losing their caressing innocence by degrees as they tightened and would not, despite her frantic struggling, let go? He said it was about release intensified by constriction, that when she came it would be her whole body letting go. Maybe the feeling of near-suffocation was more emotional than visceral and she had conjured the feeling herself as a warning—cut and run before it's too late. John, she believed, was someone capable of going too far, had probably done so with illegals he had captured. But as she stood there on Vermont Street in the aftermath of the accident, when the nameless man was taken away in the unhurried ambulance because he was beyond resuscitation, after the police had gotten her statement, after the fire truck had come to hose down the blood—after it was all over she returned, shaking, to her car to wait for John. It was his name and number that had been in her address book under "In Case of Emergency" and this, finally, was one. She had only been in El Paso a few months, working for INS. A desk job, for the most part, maintaining a database on immigration status for the constant flow from Juarez. There was really no one else but John she knew well enough to call.

After he got there he led her to his car—"Don't try to drive yours—we can come back tomorrow for it," he said, taking her in hand. She turned to him in the dark, in the green cockpit glow of the dashboard lights and the square of solid red for the unreleased brake. She wanted to say, in retrospect, "Don't let me get into my car. Don't let me hit that man because I'm running scared from you."

In his living room she wrenched off her clothes. The spots of blood on the sleeves were not her own. She drew him to her there on the floor because she couldn't wait any longer, because she believed he still might be capable of tenderness in the aftermath of an emergency. What she wanted was shelter, the certainty of his weight riding above her. But what it felt like was impact, all her bones bent to breaking beneath him, the breath driven from her lungs, her heart seized with a sickening fear that the next beat could be the next to the last. "Stop!" she said, terrified, but it was too late. She'd already let go just like he'd said. But it wasn't like he said. It was a humiliating kind of death while her body fought for breath.

In the morning she left before he woke, took her keys once and for all. She never saw him again.

The officer in charge of the case had told her the next day that the man she killed had been identified. He had been living as a permanent resident in an independent living project in a hotel that had once been marked for demolition. The residents were doing the renovation themselves. She got the number of the hotel and spoke to a Father Alvarado, who had sponsored him, and who helped supervise the construction. He said Eduardo was the man's name, that he had come from El Salvador.

"How much do you want to know?" Father Alvarado asked.

"All you can tell me," she said, but then immediately felt afraid. Hearing his name had been hard enough. Father Alvarado told her that Eduardo had been spirited across the border by the Sanctuary Movement. Spirited, as if he drifted across borders looking for a body to inhabit in a freer world.

In the hotel, he had laid tile in the bathrooms though he was far too slow by commercial standards. His right hand had been broken by government soldiers, or at least that's the story he told about himself, and who could make a thing like that up? They broke his hand, a finger at a time, to give him time to think, an incentive to tell all, to not hold anything back. They wanted the details—who he knew, where the guerillas met, what was said. They believed he was lying when he said he knew nothing. "They worked very hard to make him remember," Father Alvarado said.

She had arranged to meet Father Alvarado at the hotel. Alice wanted to see Eduardo's room, to at least look through its window. She hadn't thought this through, not really. In a way, she felt like an adopted child searching for clues that signified who he was. She wanted to know exactly whom she'd killed.

She hadn't counted on feeling so dangerous beneath the stares of his coworkers and friends. "So you're the one," their faces seemed to say, as if she'd taken a gun and shot him point blank. But eventually she moved past them, down a long hallway thick with a mist of plaster dust and a vapor of paint fumes to the room where Father Alvarado was hanging sheetrock. He was a young priest in blue jeans and a black shirt, a dark beard curling over his white clerical collar. He had a crude silver crucifix around his neck and a massive ring of keys clipped to his belt loop next to a retractable tape measure. Safety glasses shielded his eyes. He seemed to know who she was immediately. She thought he could probably sense a confession coming a mile away; she hoped her face would not betray her. She had come to look, not to tell.

He lifted his safety glasses. He looked like an aviator getting out of a biplane, his vision trying to rapidly adjust from cloud to ground. She had told him on the phone she wanted to see Eduardo's room but he seemed puzzled by her presence and she did not want to repeat this request to his face—it was hard enough to ask the first time. He wiped his hands on his jeans, leaving a white, dusty smudge like flour on his thighs. He simply placed his left hand on her right shoulder and guided her toward the stairs.

On the second floor they walked down a long hallway of num-bered rooms. He stopped in front of number eight and frowned. The door was partly open. He stepped cautiously into the room while she watched from the hallway. Bureau drawers had been wrenched from their wooden frame and were empty. The closet was bare. Only a pair of boots remained—one heel stacked at least an inch higher than the right—useless for the even-legged man who had taken his clothes. Father Alvarado gave a long sigh. "I wish they would have waited a little longer." He motioned her into the room. She tiptoed in. Somehow it seemed proper to do so.

Her eyes went immediately to the wall above the bed—a foot-high crucifix displayed its human decoration—an emaciated, bleeding Christ carved of wood, but instead of his head hanging, resigned and forsaken, he looked up, as if in the act of asking a question. He looked, not anguished like all the images of Christ she'd seen, but surprised, as if he couldn't believe the way things had turned out.

"He carved that himself," Father Alvarado said.

She nodded. She knew.

There was a picture on the dresser in a wooden frame. Two figures. She approached it slowly as if the people there would sud-denly avert their faces from the directness of her gaze. One of them was Eduardo. She would know him anywhere. And the woman—she could only be his mother. He is grinning—he knows what the camera is, but his mother looks instead at him. Or maybe she did know and wanted the picture to record that look so that he could always feel her gaze upon him from so far away. The photograph was proof—he had been alive, he had been born of a woman who clearly loved him. It felt suddenly to her that the building rolled beneath her feet. She wished it was an earthquake that made her grab for the wall. She jerked her head around to see if Father Alvarado had felt it too, was bracing himself in the door for the aftershock. But it was only her own body, seismic with guilt and dread. Father Alvarado looked at her, concerned.

"Please—I'd like to be alone for a moment here—you under-stand."

His head slowly nodded in affirmation. He was, after all, in the business of understanding. "I'll be downstairs if you need me."

She closed the door when his footsteps died away. She turned again to the bed, looked at it a long time. Then, she balanced on her right foot and slipped off her left shoe. She slipped off her right, nearly losing her balance as she did so. She steadied herself, walked barefoot across the naked wood floor leaving dark sweaty footprints in the dusty surface. She sank slowly onto the mattress. She stared at the ceiling, at the once-true squares now curling at the corners. It looked a lot like the linoleum in her mother's kitchen in San Francisco, and for a moment she felt turned upside down, as if she lay on the ceiling and was staring down at the floor.

Beneath her she felt the shape his body had carved into the mattress. She tilted her head back, took in the feet nailed to the cross, the long lean legs flowing upward toward the arching ribcage, the spread arms, the neck thrusting the head upward—the whole body a white slender flame straining to stay lit, the word "why" the wick that kept him burning against the indifferent gaze of his father who'd forsaken him.

She made herself memorize it—the last thing Eduardo saw each and every night in America, the first thing he saw in the morn-ing. Something to superimpose on the image of his face, as if see-ing what he saw could return him to his own bed once and for all, that she could then rise up, return to her own bed and safely sleep.

She lost the rhythm of her life, her habits fading from her like words on a page left too long in the sun. Sleep stopped coming alto-gether, leaving her stranded, a passenger waiting for a train that has been shunted onto another track. And she felt a huge loss—she had always loved to sleep, had enjoyed vivid dreams of weightlessness or flying, or erotic sex. But she began to have a waking dream, or a memory, she didn't know which. An image arose from the night of the accident that she had forgotten. Moments afterward a porch light went on at the nearest house. Someone stood silhouetted in the open doorway, a hall light on behind. She had shouted to call an ambulance. The person closed the door and disappeared inside the house. The moment after Eduardo had closed his eyes for the last time she ran toward that house. But before she reached its steep stairs, a woman appeared, a woman who came and put her arms around her and—did she imagine this part?—rocked her, saying over and over, "*Ay Dios mío, pobrecita, Ay Dios mío,*" a soothing incantation. Then she heard the ambulance in the distance. "Who are you?" she finally asked when she pulled back from the soft press of the woman's arms and the scent of wood smoke mixed with gardenia perfume in her clothes. "Lupita," she said. But Alice knew that angels always had aliases. She'd sat through two showings, back to back, of *Wings of Desire,* which confirmed what she'd always suspected, that angels were ambivalent, torn by the world they presided over, pulled by passions and concerns they could not always keep safe distances from. Lupita vanished when the police came. Whoever she was, she didn't want to be identified as a witness. She had only come to comfort and disappear.

Eduardo's family had been contacted in El Salvador. She waited for the phone to ring, for an anguished accusing voice in Spanish, but no call ever came. Alice's insurance company reported that all his mother wanted was his body to be shipped back to his country for burial. The insurance company, only too relieved to comply, had gotten off easy with such a modest request. So Eduardo was prepared and boxed and shipped south to his family, his country that probably he had every good reason in the world to leave but now he was returned, like a soldier from a senseless, undeclared war in the free country he'd fled to.

Then it was like the accident never happened, except that it still continued to change everything. Alice chose to see this as an omen. She waited for another sign. She wished she could open a fortune cookie that contained a clear itinerary. Go here. Do this. She would be glad for such direction. She thought of a pelican she had seen once as she drove the interstate in southern Arizona. It had been standing on the shoulder of the highway, lifting its feet one at a time from the burning pavement in a heart-wrenching dance. How could it let itself get so far away from water? Why was it just standing there, why in the world didn't it save itself and fly away?

The car had stayed on Vermont Street where she'd left it, collecting a sheaf of tickets that fluttered from their windshield-wiper binding. One day she watched a city tow truck take it. She felt strangely satisfied that the real culprit had finally been shackled and led away.

She walked down Vermont Street often. A strange name for a street in a desert town. Only a few trees, many stucco houses. For several weeks the skid marks remained—a black hieroglyphic whose meaning was clear only to her. And to the angel, Lupita, if she was still around to see it. Alice found herself looking for Lupita, searching the windows of houses up and down the low hills.

One day she followed a woman who looked like Lupita to a laundromat. Alice watched through the window as the woman settled into one of the orange plastic chairs to watch the television that was chained to a shelf. A hand-lettered sign hung from it saying "Do not Change Channels Or Volume. Thank You The Management." The woman didn't seem to have any laundry—the machines were all silent. Alice's vision telescoped. She was watching the woman through a window who was watching a program on a TV screen and on the screen was a woman looking at a smaller TV screen on which a woman could be seen climbing out a window. For Alice, time stopped. There was only this endless repetition of women and windows onto infinitesimally smaller screens.

The sun emerged briefly from the swirl of thick haze, throwing Alice's shadow on the linoleum floor right at the woman's feet.

The woman slowly turned her head to look directly at who was behind her. Alice held her breath. She waited to be recognized. But it was not Lupita, at least she didn't think so. She wore her hair young—long and loose, but the face the dark hair framed seemed at least middle-aged, and she sat with her hands on her widespread knees, reigning over the substantial territory of her lap like some Aztec priestess. She motioned to Alice to come in, but Alice froze, as if she had been caught and was about to be reprimanded. She walked quickly away from the window, turned the corner, and headed down the hill, her heart racing. She knew she needed to go back—after all, the woman had summoned her. But she needed to bring some laundry with her—she couldn't just go in empty-handed. Bringing laundry would give her something to do in the event that she had mistaken the woman's gesture.

When she came back the woman was still there. Alice glanced at her as she put a load of sheets into a machine, but the woman was intent on the television. Alice shut the lid on the roar of water, and she sat down at the opposite end of the row of chairs.

Alice hated TV, the whole blaring catalog of things for sale spliced with lean bits of entertainment; she preferred the sheltered calm of public radio. This woman seemed transfixed by it. At 4:00, the worst began—people bearing their private horrors, weeping, terrifyingly vulnerable in front of live audiences who seemed ready to have their minds changed by whichever side told the best story. The woman was rapt while a father of four told how he'd found his wife in bed with his own father. His wife calmly explained to the camera that she regarded what she did as an act of mercy, that her father-in-law had been impotent and alone ever since his wife died and she believed if she did not intervene with that kind of tenderness he would have killed himself in complete despair.

"*Ay Dios Mío!*" the woman cried, clearly angry, not with the wife but with the jeering audience.

Alice stared at her. Those same words the angel spoke that night on Vermont Street.

On the Donoghue show a woman reluctantly talked about her bulimia. Her husband, a therapist, seemed to be leading her through this public ordeal, as if disclosure was part of his prescription for her recovery.

As Alice listened to story after story, stopping only once to transfer the sheets to the dryer, she was struck by the nakedness of these confessions, the mesmerized witnessing by the audience, elevating the whole experience to some kind of religious ceremony. These TV programs might replace the Catholic Church—people, it seemed, could be absolved or damned right there on camera. She imagined herself in such a situation, sitting there and saying into a microphone for all the world to hear, "I killed someone—it was an accident." Would they jeer or weep? What part of the story would be true? How much would she have to fill in, make up, to keep their interest and their sympathy? In what way could she make it a better story?

Alice broke out in a cold sweat, felt her stomach clench and heave. She leaned forward and put her head between her knees.

"*Trágico*," the woman said, touching Alice's shoulder, mistaking her reaction as a response to the man on a commercial preview for Emergency 911. He was crying, said he'd accidentally shot his son coming through a window at night, thinking it was a burglar. The son had forgotten his keys.

"Sometimes," the woman said, switching to English without effort, "these stories seem far away, like they could never happen to you, but they're so close, if not for God's mercy you could be up there, telling it all, too."

Alice looked up, turned her whitened face toward her. "Those stories—do you think they're true?"

The woman shrugged. "True enough." She looked over at Alice's dryer, which had just stopped spinning. She got up and headed toward it. She opened the door and took out the sheets, clutching them tightly to her chest as she crossed the aisle to the counter. She set them down and began to fold.

"Wait—you don't have to do that!" Alice said, rushing over.

"This is what I do."

"For money—I mean, do you work here?"

"No, not money. I just like to do it, watch the television, talk to the people." She smoothed her large palm across a yellow pillowcase. "The clothes are warm. They're clean again. It's good."

She shook out one of the sheets, then tucked it beneath her chin. "You are not married," she said.

"How do you know?" Alice was feeling naked now, all her laundry spread out, being read like so many tea leaves.

"Single sheets—one set," the woman said, tucking the fitted sheet's gathered corners expertly together. "You may have sheets but you don't sleep," the woman said, looking at Alice sympathetically.

"You can tell that from the sheets?"

"No," the woman said, "I tell that from your eyes."

Alice's hand went involuntarily to her face, where the signs of sleeplessness were as telltale as a scar. She let her arm drop.

The words came out of her brain directly, without passing through the filter of her mind, more calmly than she would have thought possible. "I killed someone," she said. She fully expected the woman to say, "I know," as if this fact of her life, too, was in the sheets, in the features of her face.

The woman gasped, took a half-step back.

"Your husband?" she whispered.

Alice shook her head. The woman seemed to assume that murder was too intimate for complete strangers.

"Your lover?"

Alice considered this, looked away from her, let her gaze turn toward the window for a second, as if some vision might be reflected to guide her, but she saw only her own bewildered face. Should she lie, should she tell a different story? It would be appallingly easy. What if Eduardo had been her lover? She had, after all, been in his bed beneath the crucified Jesus. From there it was only a small stretch of the imagination to see herself helping him with his shirt buttons because his broken hands were more hurried than his affliction would allow. But she couldn't go any farther. Because it was someone else's story? She stayed there in his little room, unable to go forward, to consummate such an improbable love, or return to the fact of her life in a laundromat at that moment having said only a single sentence which could lead anywhere and a woman waiting breathless, for the rest.

The woman's voice brought her back from the dark comfort of Eduardo's small room to the neon-lit laundromat. "Did he hurt you?" the woman asked, leaning in slightly, as if the terrible beauty of a story of self-defense only needed coaxing.

"Yes," Alice said, shocked and oddly excited by what she was suddenly capable of.

"A gun—a knife?" The woman did not ask this eagerly. They were into the details now, the things that make it all too real, that can be held up in a court of law as concrete evidence.

A lover. Who had hurt her. His touch too brutal? His touch nonexistent and therefore just as cruel? It was an old, old story.

Alice looked at the woman, knowing the next cue would come from her face. Alice would leave and never see this woman again. She could say anything, anything at all and still walk away free, maybe freer than when she came.

Another lost image surfaced from that night, one difficult to remember until now, now that she'd summoned him. That moment before the angel Lupita came to her. Eduardo had closed his eyes. Alice could feel him slipping away. Frantic, she bent closer, listened for his heart, then brought her mouth to his and breathed, finding the rhythm, her deep breath a loud whisper that reached all the way inside to call him back. She felt him take his own first breath as if she had been the one that taught him to live. She pulled away slightly, and then he opened his eyes. That's what she could never forget, the way he'd looked at her then. Like a lover.

"He died in my arms," she said, urged on by the woman's tears that had been summoned to the corners of her eyes and waited only to fall.

She continued, emboldened now, so close to an unplanned revelation whose meaning she dared not reach too quickly. She needed to fully understand. "I wanted him to know I was the one. I wanted him to see my face, *mine*, and remember it. Always."

The woman reached for her hand. Alice hesitated, then held out her hand, palm open, to receive her.

She felt herself drifting into the night and the broken glass and the rain to look once more. This time, when she looked at Eduardo she felt herself fall slowly, face first, until she completely slipped inside him. She felt the excruciating pressure as she turned herself carefully around inside a body that was seconds away from death. She looked with him, at the shape of herself bending close. A face he might have created, a face that had waited in wood for him to release its true human expression, tender and astonished, exactly like his own.

Last Call at the Next-Best Western

Miller Time. That's what the sign over the bar says. If I could change it it would say Tornado Time, any minute now. The sky on the way to work this afternoon was blue-black tinged with green, like a brand-new bruise from an old argument. If Dorothy's still in Kansas, if she won't go looking beyond her own back yard for her heart's desire, then send the storm south to me. I'm ready to be lifted up, blown right on out of Oklahoma. Over the rainbow? It's not far enough from here. Beyond the beyond is where I really need to be.

The Pabst Blue Ribbon sign fires right up when I plug it in, and the sky blue waters start rolling over the rocks. I listen hard but I can't hear the river, only the June bug buzz of the fluorescent tube behind it. I lean back against the bar and stare at it. I'm facing eight whole hours of pouring shots and pulling drafts, slicing lemons and limes, jamming toothpicks into the olives. There's no end in sight.

This place used to be a Best Western, but was sold off a few months back. The Patel's bought it. Cash. A couple from India expecting their first kid. "There goes the neighborhood," the guy who owns the car wash next door said. But the Patels have actually improved the place. Or tried to. They lit incense and put flowers and fruit and a bowl of rice on the doorstep, maybe to get the bad spirits out. I don't think it worked. Then they put up a big sign that says Muskogee Budget Lodge, all the letters working. I still call it the Best Western, even though it's only next best. Right below it, the sign says, "Chief Buffalo's Musical Memory Lane." We don't have a chief, and Buffalo's real name is Rocky LaRue. He's only *from* Buffalo, upstate New York. But I guess the Patels think it looks good on the marquee.

It's just perfect. The perfect place for me. The joke of Muskogee. The Patels can't help it that I can't stand it here. My whole life, for the most part, has truly sucked, and I've been happy maybe for a total of six or seven hours in it. It all started the day I was born. I know I got mixed up with the baby next to me in the hospital. That's what my daddy said. He leaned over my crib and said, "Where did this little Injun come from? Not from me." That other girl, the whiter one, is out there somewhere living a real life, probably with a trust fund to boot, not with the other single moms humping for minimum wage in the casino or blowing their wages for the big jackpot in the sky.

My mother got me this dream job a few months ago. A step up from the casino, at least. She won the Mary Kaye hot pink Cadillac for being saleswoman of the year ten years ago. Now her Cadillac has faded to the color of baby aspirin tablets you spilled and forgot at the bottom of your purse, barely pink any more. Serves her right. I guess she thought she was doing me a favor, trying to make up for things that can't ever be set right. Or maybe this is my fate for not letting old scores be settled. Some things just don't settle, even over time.

If it weren't for Buffalo I couldn't stand this place. I call him my medicine man as a joke. He sometimes gives me extra Valium he gets from the VA for PTSD. Some part of his brain is still in Pearl Harbor hearing the planes come in from Japan.

Buffalo, who's not even an Indian, let alone a chief, presides over the Musical Memory Lane: a table stacked with cassette tapes, all labeled and systemitized according to year. He puts pencils and index cards on all the tables and you write down what you want to hear. He knows the history of the song—who wrote it, who else recorded it, who played on it, what movie it was in.

The regulars who come here have known him for years, but the strangers who sometimes show up for sales conferences don't believe a seventy-year-old man will have anything they want to listen to and they're mostly right. But they're surprised when they put things like U2 and Nirvana on their lists and he's got it all. He even has an obscure country song I happen to love called "If I'd Shot You When I Met You I'd Be Out of Jail by Now." I wish I'd written it. I've *lived* that song.

So here comes Buffalo, pushing through the emergency exit door. He looks both excited and worried sick, an expression on his face like he's just read his horoscope and it told him his ship is coming in but there's a nuclear submarine in the way with all its torpedoes pointed in his direction. Maybe the tornado's on the edge of town by now. Not a minute too soon in my book.

He stops in front of the bar, looks up at me, and says, "Faith, they've got karaoke at the new Best Western up in Tulsa now. We're done for unless we make some changes around here."

"That's cheating," I say. "They're too cheap to hire a real band."

He looks at me like I just came in from Mars. I shrug and fill the sink with hot, soapy water, dunk the rest of last night's glasses in the rinse.

Buffalo gathers up a handful of creamers, those tiny tubs of half-and-half, and opens them up and pours them into a dish and sets it out for the stray cat and her kittens who live out behind the pool house. It nearly broke my heart the first time I saw him do it, seeing those kittens come running like he was their mama and truly cared whether they went hungry or not. The mama cat never does show herself, but you can feel her watching to make sure there isn't any danger. She crouches out there in the dark and waits until he leaves before she'll come for the cream.

When Buffalo opens the back door the sky is a creepy color, yellow now and deathly still. I may get my wish, after all. But the sirens haven't gone off so it could mean nothing.

He goes back to his table and slides a box out from under it. He opens it up and stares at whatever's in there.

"So what's in the box, Chief?" I call him that sometimes when he needs cheering up.

"Technology," he answers, tapping on the box. He lifts out a metal thing about two feet long and six inches high. He sets it on the table, takes out a little keyboard, and plugs it in the back.

"Battery powered, too," he notes with pride. "Are you watching?"

"Can't take my eyes off it," I say. It hardly seems worth all the fuss. He types something on the keyboard and the next thing I know there's red letters streaming across the box, which is really a kind of screen. The letters are flashing on and off. "Hi, Faith!" it says. I can't believe how totally ridiculous it is.

"My name in lights after all this time," I say, trying not to sound sarcastic. Who's he kidding with this thing? But he's excited; he's on a roll now. He's typing out other things: "No Rap, No Heavy Metal. All the Songs You Want to Hear." He's so happy with this gadget. He actually thinks he's going to head karaoke off at the pass. And as I watch his face, full of pride, I can see real hope behind it, and I have to admit that hope, when it's aimed at something, can be a powerful thing.

There's a two-bit telemarketing convention from Ponca City in town, and the bar is filling up with strangers. So I'm almost disappointed when my mother doesn't show. She's been in here a lot lately, drinking her club sodas with lime. She's tried to get me in on Mary Kaye, but I couldn't take it, all those makeovers. It's not that easy to become a new person, even a better-looking one. I've got scars that won't fade. And the same old resentments are etched deep in my brain.

The people from Com-Tel look worn out from all the pep rallies in the meeting room and are ready to party, but they look definitely shocked when they walk in. "Where's the karaoke?" some asshole shouts. "All the songs you want to hear," Buffalo types out hopefully on his sign. But nobody seems to see it, and if they do they blow it off. Buffalo tries to get them to make requests, but they seem bored or annoyed when he comes up to their tables and explains what the pencils and cards are for. A layer of smoke settles down and through it Buffalo's red sign streams bravely along.

I hear the tornado siren before he does. He's right by the speakers, and I make a whirling motion in the air with my hand as a signal. Usually he shuts down the music, but tonight he types out a message, just like they do at the bottom of your TV screen so as not to interrupt the show. The words "Tornado Warning" stream across the sign in capital letters. It's wonderful. Nobody pays attention and the one guy who does, the one who's leaning to starboard on the stool in front of me, says, "Hey, Pocohontas!"

My hackles go up. You sonofabitch. "If I had an Indian name it would be Cuts With a Knife. No one would mess with me then, especially you."

He only smirks, happy to get a rise out of me. My hair I can bleach out but not my eyes. They stay dark, dark as outer space no matter what color contacts you put in. A throwback, my mother says I am, to my full-blood grandmother. Throwback sounds like something you do to undersize trout. Nothing worth keeping. Her name was Annie Tenkiller. Now there's a *name*.

"Tornado Warning," the guy says to me, trying to focus on Buffalo's sign. "I never heard of that band before. Are they from around here?"

"Yeah. They're about to blow you away." And he still doesn't get it. He writes down on one of the cards, "Anything by Tornado Warning," and takes it over to Buffalo. Buffalo just looks at the guy after he's read the card. He looks around the room and realizes nobody's even paying attention to the sign, and if they are they're too loaded to read it. The sirens, there's more of them now so we know they mean business, cut through. It isn't a warning any more. It's here.

Some idiot opens the fire exit door to look through the doorway, and we can all see it beyond the pool, a funnel cloud coming down like a finger, like a great big accusation pointing straight down at Muskogee, then there's a crash like two locomotives colliding as it touches ground and keeps on coming.

The kittens streak into the room, their tails like bottle brushes,

and Buffalo runs over to the door to close it and yells at everyone to
get under whatever they can. We all crouch down on the floor
beneath the tables, which seems silly since they're pedestal tables and
most of them are so un-level they're balanced with matchbooks and
Sweet and Low packets to keep them steady. Right next to me the
kittens are hissing at each other as if one of them is the cause of it
all. The lights go out and it's Buffalo's red sign that stands out now,
running on batteries. "Tornado Warning" streams on. The guy at
the bar got what he deserved. You can feel it in the air, the pressure,
and I don't mean barometric. Most of us get quiet but we're all looking at ourselves real hard now; some of us don't like what we see.

The latest argument I had with my mother on the phone this
morning comes back to me with the volume on high, above the roar.
She says she won't loan me any money for a vacation, that I made
my bed and now I'm going to have to lay in it. She should know.
She spent half of my Wonder Years in jail while I was farmed out to
her friend Sue Ann.

When I was little I hated my mother for being in jail. Sue Ann
and I would go to visit her on Sundays, talk on a black phone and
look through a window that had chicken wire in it and talk about
how she didn't mean to kill my father, that she was only trying to
protect me. From what? They lied to me, both of them. My mother
was only in for *attempted* murder, unbeknownst to me. Sue Ann,
it turns out, paid my father to leave town after he got out of the
hospital. He didn't need to be asked twice. He'd already gambled
away the house and the car. So I grew up thinking he was in heaven
when he was really in Las Vegas. For five hundred bucks he gladly
gave up being a father. I guess I wasn't worth fighting for. Eight
years later Sue Ann and I went to pick up my mother at the jail.
She came through the gate with a grocery sack with her clothes in
it and her hair black and long. I started crying and said, "That's
not her. That's not my mama." She got in the car and she started
crying too and tried to hug me. I jumped out of the car and started
running down the road. They followed me in the car, honking for

me to stop but it only made me run faster. Finally I couldn't run any more and just sat down in the road. Sue Ann had to slam on the brakes. My mother got out of the car and sat down, too. We cried for a while. I don't remember who stopped first. I don't think either of us has cried since.

Why do I suddenly feel so strange? I've been through a lot of tornadoes before. I don't know why this one should be any different. An hour ago I was rooting for it. Now, every nerve in my body is on fire and there's nowhere to run. I put my head down, get into the crash position.

Between the flashes of lightning Buffalo has moved in closer toward me, and just as he gets within range, one of my hands shoots out and grabs him. Between that flash and the next, I've got a hold of Buffalo's hand. He's all I've got right now. There isn't any more time.

I'd hold my mother's hand just like this if she were right here, if she'd let me. But it's hard to even imagine that kind of closeness with her. She always says I could have made something of myself if I'd tried harder. If I die tonight, what would my tombstone say? "Here Lies Faith. She Tried." It wasn't enough for either of us.

Somewhere in the middle of it someone gets on her mobile phone and says, "Honey, I'm scared." At least she's got somebody to call. Somebody to call honey that likes to hear her say it. Somebody to admit to that she's about to shit her pants. All I've got is the hand of a seventy-year-old man, and he can't ease the pain no matter how much Valium he sends my way.

Six o'clock. I hear someone's digital watch beeping behind me. Tornado Warning still streams across the sign. It should be saying, "The End is Near," because it surely is.

Buffalo lets go of my hand. He makes his way back to the keyboard. He flicks a lighter but he looks like he can't think of anything to type. The lighter goes out. Someone cries and someone else swears and some guy behind me prays out loud. Buffalo is deathly still and I want to say something to all of them. That's when

I think of Norma Rae in the movie writing the union sign and climbing up on the table and holding it above her head daring people to say otherwise. One word could change everything.

"Listen!" is what I finally shout into that dark room full of people. *Listen.* It means a lot of things. Listen to your heart or the breathing of the person next to you. Listen to your mother—she might need to tell you something that could save your life. Listen to music from now on as if you really have to hear it, as if it could be the very last song coming down the line.

But what I hear is something scratching at the door.

I crawl over to the door, push against it and it swings hard, nearly coming off the hinges.

From where I'm still sitting on the floor I can see her—the mama cat, crouched, eyes wide as saucers just watching me and a kitten that isn't moving held in her mouth.

The wind starts to die down. The sky, almost out of purple, is about to let the blue back in. But the pool chairs are flung all over, the cushions floating in the water. The roof of the motel peels back like a sardine tin. I doubt the Patels can fix it. If they have any sense they'll burn it down.

Some dickhead yells out the door, "Bartender, line 'em up, it's time to celebrate! We survived!"

I don't even turn around. I walk slowly toward the cat and she isn't moving, just staring at me with her ears flat back. Her whole body listens. I lower myself down on one knee and hold out my hand. I don't have a bowl of cream, just myself. What will it mean if she comes to me? She doesn't come any closer, but she doesn't run. She actually puts the kitten down. Like an offering. It starts moving. She holds her ground and waits as if she knows that sooner or later the bowl of cream will come again. Close enough to actually see the person who offers it, close enough to let us see that she'll let herself want it. She knows it's what she has to have, sooner or later. A cat that might have had a name once but hasn't heard it in a very long time.

The two kittens that have been hiding behind the bar run between my feet toward their mother, toward their sister or brother. It's the first time I hear a sound from her, a high-pitched cry, a homing signal.

Mrs. Patel opens the back door of the restaurant and steps into the wind. Her purple sari fills like a sail, her belly underneath round as the moon with a baby swimming in it. She sees me and lifts her hand, not in greeting, but in weary surrender. Then Mrs. Patel turns and goes back inside, her sari billowing behind her.

How do you go back to the world when there's so much to make right? What do *I* want? Who do I think I am? I used to think I wanted to be a singer. I stopped trying when I was ten. My mother said I didn't have any range, that I couldn't even make the Methodist choir. Right now, if I could still sing I'd do it, like the mockingbird up on the power pole my daddy used to go out and throw rocks at in the middle of the night. I'd sing my brains out, song after song after song, everything I ever heard, all of what I knew or dreamed about until something out there answered me. Until my mother would sing with me again like she did when I was little, when she was still somebody I could look up to.

The lights go on again and the last song queued up blares from the speakers. "Proud to Be an Okie from Muskogee." We always save it for last call. Tonight, Buffalo turns the volume way down. Nothing lasts: bad storms and dead-end jobs, what we've come to think of as safe and solid, good songs we thought would last forever.

The rain starts counting, drops at first, then sheets, until the surface of the pool shatters with water. The mother cat and kittens race for shelter. There's just me, trying to remember the prayer my mother taught me. *If I die before I wake.* What comes after? No Rap. No Heavy Metal. I listen to the wind and Merle Haggard, hold on for an answer.

West of Rain

He blames the light. The edges of the wedding pictures curl inward, tighten toward a scroll. He blames the heat, too. And sweat from carrying it all up the mountain on his back, a box, a board at a time until this small structure here, this one laid out on the flat top of the mesa, began to look something like a house. This afternoon his son stands below with a bucket, looks up once, shading his eyes, at his father on the edge then turns toward the water, the black dog following close behind.

Just the two of them now, and the dog. He watches the boy, the one who came out of the hill country, that place with live oak and shade. His mother's needs were hidden at the time. Now, everything's out in the open; nothing but creosote and ocotillo to throw their spindly shade on the bare bentonite hills. The dog stops once to bite a sticker from its paws, shakes his head to free it from his tongue. His son threads his way easily through all of it to the spring.

The father had dug the spring out of rock and clay with a shovel, believing in the water that was surely staunched behind, felt sure it would show once he went deep enough. He found the crevice clogged with stones, the taproots of desperate mesquite. They were once a decent height, the trees, before the miners came; now they grew like snakeweed, clinging to the cliff and each other. A year of digging, and then the water came, a miracle he couldn't claim. He wasn't ready yet to call it a sign.

The son stops at the overflowing stock tank, bends to drink, then dunks his whole head under. He comes up dripping and the bees resting on the tank's rim start to zing around him. The father can't see the bees from where he stands on the end of the mesa, but he knows how they do when disturbed. They buzz like the bright ideas the boy's always having. Lately, he wants to pierce his ear.

The father goes back to the half-finished house. Dust stirs as he opens the door and the pictures scatter like dry leaves on the bed, curl tighter as he watches. White clothes, dirty now. She was a handful, even then. Beautiful. She could ride the hair off a horse. And him. The last time he saw her was in the headlights coming home to the other house, the one in the ghost town. She was standing on the side of the road, her arm raised, not for a ride, but for a blow she was just about to deliver to the boy, six then. Because the dog shit in the house. Or the wind drove her crazy. Or she couldn't get enough. That lush place inside herself dry as devil's claw, the shed carapace of a centipede curled like a tiny ear. Nothing left to drink and the kid wanting his say with the dog because it was his. His.

A cane of ocotillo was what she had in her hand. He could see it as he drove toward them. She was numb to the thorns and the dog cowered and barked, not yet hit but remembering how it felt before they took him from the shelter.

He yanked on the emergency brake, leapt out of the truck. Shouted at her to stop as he ran toward them. She turned in the headlights, her hand bloody from gripping the branch. She looked at her hand, not him, surprised that she bled, that she had something left to bleed with. That's how desiccated she was by then. Like the thorny stick she held. A desert thing determined to scratch if touched, bent on teaching a lesson. Why wasn't once enough? Why did she have to go on making a point? Why was the boy so stubborn?

She came at her husband and there was nothing to do but tackle her. The dog went crazy, wanting to bite but didn't. The boy held it back with both arms as the father covered the mother, pinned her to the ground.

The moon floated up behind the Chisos, dragging a cloud along like a shy girl about to drop a towel. Everything had a shadow now. He heard her breathing hard as if they had just made love.

The engine in the truck throbbed with what little gas was left, a cylinder missing. It stuttered, died, shook itself like the dog when wet. The headlights burned on for a time and the dog stopped barking. She quit breathing so hard.

He could hear the radio then, the last of a *cumbia*. A long pause as the DJ fumbled for another CD. An orchestra, of all things. Big Sky Music. The theme from *Shane*. Over it, the DJ howled.

She wasn't fighting any more. He didn't have anything she wanted. He raised himself off her, saw her bloody left hand, the thick lashes that never needed makeup. She looked through that black fringe at him. He was tired of caring who won.

"Are you happy now?" he asked. It was a real question. She might have been. He didn't wait for an answer. "I'm taking him."

The radio died. The lights. The truck. The love. Is that what it was? Or just luck, gone under?

The boy held onto the dog. It was what he had that was his.

She sat up. The dog broke free of the boy and came to her, licked her hand. She let it. "See?" she seemed to say. "There's something every living thing has to have, sooner or later. Some of us know where to get it." She kicked the dog away.

She pushed herself up from the ground, leaving a handprint in the dirt. He'd look for it and not find it the next day, the place where she traded the son for whatever could still feed her.

The boy didn't hear what she said. He was already walking down the road, the dog running to catch up. The house where they lived, where she would not be going back to, was half a house to begin with, stuck together from adobe and wood. Some miner had lived there when the mine was full of cinnabar, squeezing quicksilver from the ore down at Study Butte smelter before the veins tapped out. They didn't know back then it could kill you, that the shiny, heavy liquid could do more than rise or fall in glass thermometers. A slow death from something with such a pretty name. A secret hazard.

The father feels the new house taking shape. He's built it solid and square and true. Two houses this time. The one on top of the mesa for music, the one below for living in. The son has his own room and he'll be sleeping in it soon, his pierced ear tuned toward the music up the mountain. How will he think about love, find out what his body can do? The father finds other uses for his hands. Just last week he taught his son a chord.

The boy starts back now with the bucket of water. It sloshes in the pail and the dog tries to drink it before it hits the ground, red tongue licking air.

The father takes the guitar from the black case. There's time to play a song before the boy and the dog get back with the water. Time to stretch his scarred, rough hands over seven frets. Six strings, like the Chinese hexagram. The Cauldron. The Well. No changing lines. This is it, right here. The light left on the Chisos when the sun goes. The brisket of Willow Mountain. Sienna. Rose madder. Burnt umber. The colors of the photographs on the bed are nothing now, wedding clothes fading from white to gray, to black.

But there was one more night after she left when he almost lost what he still had. He had been sitting at the Study Butte store, drinking and singing until they turned out the lights. It was what he came to Terlingua for—lots of beer and weed and no laws to speak of. But the boy was waiting for him and tired of waiting. Came swinging, he did. He knew how to hit; he'd seen it done. He laid into his father, who was so full of *sotol* he fell to his knees, right onto the green swords of the cactus it came from. And it finally got through—what the boy had to have. His full attention. To not be left this way again.

Okay, he said, and meant it. That he could set certain things aside, that he'd make a choice on this side of love, the kind he didn't know he had to have.

He carried the first beam near daylight, head and heart pounding, and named the hill for his son. Together they called it a mountain. Put it all down on paper and signed the deed to the land it took a thousand songs to pay for. Heads of corporations at the resort in Lajitas tipped him well to play "Streets of Laredo." He always threw in "My Funny Valentine," which they didn't much care for. And when the land was his and the boy said his own name with the word "mountain" after it his father knew the absolute truth, the breadth of what he'd given to his son. An offering of something actual.

The father puts the guitar back in the case now, goes out to wait for the boy to carry the water the rest of the way up the mountain. So much has been spilled. But when the cup is dipped down to the bottom and filled and held out to him he's so grateful he could cry. He didn't know he was this thirsty, that the water he'd found, that his son has just carried to him, is so much sweeter for the climb.

Divided Highway

Walker tries to sing against the roar of the wind that blasts through both open windows as he drives, but it comes out more like a shout. "Break on Through" accompanies him from the single dashboard speaker, buzzing with cranked-up bass. In his head, he's trying hard not to come apart.

Along the highway there are many small, crude crosses, reminders of accidents at every curve. There are flowers on some, photographs on others, but Walker is going too fast to make out the faces. Behind the Ford pickup, the Airstream fishtails as if it hates being hauled. He fully expects the hitch to break any minute and the thing will roll away on its own. He wonders what in the world he was thinking when he bought it—only an hour ago? It seems as if it has been tied to him for years.

On the seat next to him, a box. What looks like it should have held a pair of shoes holds his brother, or what's left of him. In his mind, he only knows he's starting over, and getting rid of his brother's ashes seems the first part of a plan that reveals itself to him a mile at a time. It's a plan that will lead him at last, he believes, into the present tense of his life, a place he's only drifted through repeatedly on the way back and forth.

He picked up the box at UPS in Reno, along with his brother's guitar (why his mother also sent that he could only guess), and set right out from there with a brief stop to buy the trailer in Sparks. Maybe he bought it for no other reason than the way it caught the light, a blinding light, a vision. A spaceship on wheels. And the money his mother had sent him in an envelope taped to the shoebox amounting to $986.00, the sum total of what had been in his brother's savings account, his inheritance now, was just enough to buy the trailer. When he signed over the check to the RV dealer it had been a relief. He'd wanted to get rid of the money as soon as possible. He'd hardly even looked inside the trailer, said he was in a hurry. The man who sold it to him asked him jokingly if he was being followed. For a moment, Walker almost turned to look behind him, as if the ghost of his brother might materialize right there and jinx the whole deal. He tore out of the used RV lot in a cloud of dust and sprayed gravel.

He doesn't have to think hard about where he'll take the ashes. The road reveals itself to him on the map: Pyramid Way, north out of Sparks, then east, the direction of the sun. Close enough to the desert where the Burning Man festival was to be held, where he and Lee once planned to go together. Back when plans were still something that could be made and honored. Until Lee took himself out. Shot himself twice. *Twice.* The first time he missed his heart.

A pyramid-shaped rock rises out of the desert lake like a pharaoh's tomb, massive and mysterious and pointed sharply at the broad blue sky. The famous explorer, Frèmont, had written in 1843 after a fearful journey through the nearby Blackrock Desert, "a sheet of green water . . . broke upon our eyes like the ocean" and had compared the Pyramid island to the Great Pyramid of Cheops. But when Walker finally pulls off the road and stands on a bluff north of Sutcliff, he has to squint to see it: an unremarkable, squat little rock in a blue sink, at least from that vantage point. The sun is nearly down. He doesn't have time to drive all the way around through the town of Nixon to get to a place where the scale matches the photographs. He checks his map, decides to head for the nearest place he can get to before dark, a place called The Needles on the north shore.

Bad road all the way there, washboard and sinkholes and cows sauntering across the road no matter how hard he blasts the horn. He passes a grove of tamarisk with a single picnic table lurched onto its side, a tilted trashcan, a boarded-up restroom, a bullet-riddled sign that said Campground Closed. Further on, after a mile or more of dust unfurling behind him like a tail of smoke from a rocket, he threads his way through more cows, low hills. Finally, he sees tufa spires rise, limestone formations like calcified icing dripped from some melting thing, and a roaring green fumarole spewing sulfurous fumes from an old well. Steaming water pools in muddy pockets and runs downhill where it hisses as it meets the cooler water of the lake. A fitting place for Lee's remains.

Walker gets out of the truck and dips his fingers into one of the pools, jerks back instantly. It's scalding. Down where the runoff meets the lake water, the temperature is almost bearable. He takes off his shoes and wades in.

Not a soul in sight. Pelicans cruise two inches above the water like judges in search of misdemeanors, then they veer for a small limestone island offshore where they fold themselves on the barren rock discussing their verdicts. The sun drops down below the mountains and everything that has been bleached in stark light takes on a pink cast that softens even the bony towers. The pyramid, though still stunted, turns a glorious bronze. The sand sighs, he can hear it—the relief of the sun letting go after a long, scorched day. Walker stands, transfixed. The water doesn't move, the wind doesn't stir; the birds have gone to roost. It's a moment when the world pauses and listens to itself; the hour of longing. What the Scotch called the gloaming. A word his brother, the poet, the bard, the garden variety drunk, used often to describe a state of melancholy that bordered on sweetness, a place he lingered briefly until one sip too many took him over the edge into oblivion where he seemed most at home.

He opens the shoebox that holds Lee's ashes. Inside there's a plastic bag closed with a red twistie tie. He nearly laughs. This must be the budget version of cremation, the minimum urn, he thinks wryly. He pictures a metal incinerator in the back lot of the funeral home, a janitor pushing the lid down on Lee to make him fit. The inside of the crematorium is reserved for deluxe packages with a proper receptacle at the end—people with money, impressive obituaries. He untwists the tie, hesitates, inches his fingers in. He pulls out a fistful of his brother, looks at it. Dust and grit and bits of bone no different than the crumbling limestone all around him. It's heavy, almost sticky. He tosses a handful into the water. It clouds, then sinks and settles. The water grows clear again. Walker puts the lid back on the box. What is he going to do with it? He already fought back his first impulse in Reno to toss it in the dumpster at the gas station where he'd filled up. He'd gotten past all the places he'd wanted to fling it out the window at signs that warned of five hundred-dollar fines for littering. Now he stands uncertainly on the shore of a strange lake watching the dusk pushing downward, the limned edge of the mountains like light beneath a jagged door. He only wants to be rid of it so he can go even though he has no place in mind to get to, just an unmarked place called The Rest of Your Life where he imagines he can still arrive and begin.

He wades in a little further until the bottoms of his rolled-up jeans get wet. He goes further still, up to his knees and stops. He sets the box on the water, then gives it a little push. It seems to want to float. There are no bulrushes for it to be hidden in and Lee is beyond saving now. Slowly, it drifts on some imperceptible current, an underground spring.

"Take a good, last look," Walker says, "this is the best I can do." His voice comes out thin and broken, feeble. Even so, it echoes off the drum of the still lake. He rehearsed a hundred indictments over the years but not one of them comes to mind now. A few pelicans rustle their wings but do not take flight. The box drifts. How long before it soaks and sinks? Walker doesn't stay to watch. He trudges through the water toward the beach. He turns once and sees it still floating stubbornly in the general direction of the pyramid, now a tarnished brass triangle in the leftover light.

He feels as isolated as an astronaut, the Airstream behind him a landing craft that has crashed into an asteroid beyond the reach of gravity, of noise, of earth. If he screams alone in his tin can house not a soul will hear him. He's been orbiting for years. His brother had had a telescope once. But then the moon became a walked-on place, drained of wonder. And now he's in the strangest, loneliest place on earth he's ever been; of course it's his brother who has brought him here.

He doesn't actually see the box go under but he senses it—something small dissolving into something greater. He can't say whether he likes the feeling or not. It leaves him soon enough. But he feels it, the opening of an old door to which he's always had the key: a wild hope, a genetic knack for blunder.

The trailer has lost the gleam it had in the sun's glare and now looks more pewter than silver. The door is open, the light in the cab on. A little wedge of civilization in the moonscape. From the tufa towers, movement. Wings. Bats? No, the flight's too smooth. Then he hears them. Owls, dozens of them careening around the towers, hooing mournfully, their cries echoing off the rock and the lake, hungry and hurrying the dark to flush out their prey. They are wholly unconcerned with Walker and the box that holds his brother at the bottom of Pyramid Lake.

Stars poke through, one at a time, as if someone stands on the other side of the sky shooting their way out of heaven. One star falls, gaseous and green, but not as far as Earth. Another keeps going—a satellite, maybe. A determined little blip, steady on.

The light is almost gone now. He steps inside the trailer. On the couch lies the guitar case that had belonged to his brother.

Walker lifts Lee's Gibson, his legacy, out of its case, sets it on the floor. Lee had taught him to play, which hadn't been easy. The lessons were full of mean-spirited put-downs, goadings, taunts. But Walker stuck it out. He learned to read Lee's signals, how to complement his playing and stay out of the way. By the time Walker was fourteen, Lee twenty-one, Lee took him to Winfield, Kansas, to accompany him in the flat-picking contest. It was the year a kid of nine was going to win. Easy to tell from the first round. Lee couldn't stand it. He drank himself into a stupor and when they got on stage he was only halfway through the first song when he dropped his pick on the floor. He glared at Walker and told him to pick it up. Walker didn't move. Lee shouted at him. The silence in the auditorium was awful. Finally the MC thanked them and asked them to leave the stage. "Thank you very much." It echoes, still, that amplified shame.

Walker goes back out to the truck now, rummages through the toolbox until he finds what he's looking for. In three swift strokes he nails the guitar to the pine-paneled wall in the trailer with a single nail the length of a railroad spike. He likes the way it looks. And it's necessary, like the little crosses along the road. Something happened here, it seems to say. Be careful. Pay attention. It could happen again.

Walker drives into high wind and blowing sand as he leaves highway 395, turns east on I-40. He's been in windstorms before but this could be the worst. Tumbleweeds roll and bounce across the road and cars veer wildly to avoid them. He decides to pull off, have coffee, wait to see if it blows over, figure out what to do next.

There's only one other person at the counter of the Sidewinder Cafe, an old man in a cowboy hat hunched over a cup of coffee and a piece of chocolate cream pie. Walker takes a seat three stools away from him. On the wall behind the cash register there's a gallery of snapshots taped to the pine paneling. Walker leans closer to look. Old Polaroids from some movie shoot, dollies and cranes and booms and the local folk grinning ear to ear, standing next to the German stars whose names they'd probably never heard of.

Walker orders coffee, drinks it steadily, wrapping both his hands around the mug for warmth. The old man turns slowly on his stool. Walker feels him staring. He turns his head. On the old man's sweat-stained hat, across the crown, the word TRUTH in two-inch-high letters written with a green felt-tip pen. Walker

knows the man expects him to ask, "So what's the truth?" but he
won't do it. The man continues staring. Walker stares back.

"You're dying to know, aren't you?" the man says.

"No, not particularly."

"It won't cost you a thing." He takes out a mangled cigarette
from his shirt pocket and lights it with a wooden match struck on
the bottom of the counter. The flame wavers in his shaking hands.

"OK," Walker says. "So what is the truth?"

The man takes a deep breath of smoke, holds it in, and lets it
out. Walker fully expects a hacking cough to follow but none
comes. "The truth," the man says, narrowing his eyes to get his
point across, "is in the middle of a big mistake."

The man takes another long draw on his cigarette. ". . . and
you're the only one here," he says, rising from his stool. "So it must
belong to you." He extracts a dollar from a thin billfold and lays
it on the counter, put a salt shaker on it to hold it down as if a sudden wind might take it away.

Walker nearly chokes on his coffee. He manages to swallow
most of it, then gave a short, nervous laugh. "So what should I do,
oh wise one?" he asks.

The man turns. "Now how would I know?" he says. He looks
as if he's burning to say something else but he just shrugs, gets off
the stool with some difficulty, shuffles out the door. Walker watches
through the window as he eases himself into a red and white
Rambler station wagon and drives away.

The waitress comes, takes the dollar, then pours Walker a refill.
She goes to the cash register, rings up seventy-five cents from the
man's dollar, and puts a quarter in her apron pocket. She looks at
Walker. "Piece of pie?" she asks, as if Truth might require something sweet to chase it down with.

Walker shakes his head. He stands up to leave, lays his dollar
down like a napkin to the left of his plate. He sets a fork on top of
it. As he pulls the door shut behind him, he feels dread catching
up to him. It follows him to his truck, sits down next to him like

a hitchhiker with a gun pointed at him as if waiting for an explanation he can't give, money he doesn't have.

The wind has died down a little, but not much. The moon
dissolves inside a murky pink haze on the horizon like an aspirin
tablet dropped in water. He fiddles nervously with the radio, pulls
in a strong station from Barstow, and hears a spokesman from
NASA talk about the first shuttle landing, how it might have to
make another orbit or two because of the high winds. The local
announcer says people are gathering at Edwards Air Force Base,
camping out, waiting, that it's a historic moment in the space program, in America's reach for the stars. The more Walker listens, the
more he knows he has to go.

On a little rise he looks in the rearview mirror and sees a string
of lights curving through the desert. The entrance to the AFB is
unmistakable, marked by huge lights, the kind that highway crews
use at night. Chain-link fence stretches away from the opening on
either side over hard-packed sand. Military sentries beckon him
through with flashlights. He drives toward the lights across a wide
tarmac, an unused runway, he guesses, guided to a parking spot.
There are hundreds of camper trucks, cars, motor homes in perfect formation. He shuts off the engine, the lights, and leans on
the steering wheel. Wind rocks the truck, even with the trailer
attached. He sets the brake. Above the wind he can hear a loudspeaker. He rolls down the window and listens for a while to a
woman's voice at mission control, giving a stream of constant data:
wind shear factors, trajectory speed. He gets out of the truck, walks
toward a bank of lights near the speaker. A group of people in down
coats and watch caps pulled low over their ears stand around a
makeshift kiosk drinking coffee. He thinks he hears someone say
there's a good chance the landing will be cancelled if the wind
doesn't die down.

Walker makes his way slowly up and down the rows. He keeps
looking for the Truth man's red and white Rambler but doesn't spot
it. He isn't exactly sure he likes being here. It's like being detained

at a border while some provisional government that has just pulled off a coup decides your fate. An entire population waits, corralled inside a camp, surrounded by chain-link fence and barbed wire, sentries at the gates. He begins to wonder if he'll ever get out of here. He makes his way back to his trailer, glad to see it, glad he has a place to crawl into. But now he wishes he hadn't nailed the guitar to the wall. It hangs there, silent, a black hole gaping behind the strings. The wind rocks the trailer, moans through the aluminum. The woman's voice on the loudspeaker stays steady and flat like a repeated prayer, a ribbon of sound flung forward and back, loud and faint, clear and broken by the stronger voice of the wind. He drifts in and out of sleep, feels as if he's in a metal coffin listening to the roar of bitter wind, the woman's voice repeating things that, for the life of him, he does not understand.

Walker finds himself somewhere in Louisiana again, middle of the night, 1969, in the back seat of the new Chevy. They're flying, he's sure of it. He's never felt a car move at such a speed. He's ten years old. Lee is barely eighteen, just got his driver's license. It is so dark he can barely make out the shape of his brother in the driver's seat, both hands resting easy on the wheel. The car is less than a month old, an extravagance. His mother called it Lee's Folly, but Lee saw it as an advance on a style of living he felt he deserved, already was born to, and had been unfairly kept from by circumstances beyond his control.

When the headlights of oncoming cars flood the interior for a few seconds Walker can see a bit of his brother's face in the rearview mirror. The expression is one he hasn't seen before. He looks excited, and something else, like he's getting away with murder. Walker halfway expects the police to be coming after them, sirens and whirling lights, the whole nine yards. He looks out the back every once in a while but there's nothing but the road, almost silver in the moonlight, snaking back to Biloxi. Walker is sure he's been kidnapped, abducted by his brother, who's finally taking him somewhere.

What Walker hadn't actually heard but had filtered into his sleep just the same was his brother's slow burn all evening. He'd drunk himself not into a stupor but into a state of heated resentment about a gig that had fallen through that morning at a roadhouse he'd been playing. He muttered something about teaching Walker to play so they could have a brother act. He sat in a chair in front of the television carrying on a vicious but completely coherent commentary on whatever happened to be on the screen. He leaned forward to change channels constantly. Their mother was in the bedroom trying to concentrate on her lesson plans for the next day. It was Lee's sudden silence rather than his complaints that brought her out of the room. He was leaning forward, elbows on his knees, in rapt attention at the image on the screen of the rocket at Cape Canaveral that was set for launch in the morning. He stood up abruptly and headed straight for Walker's room.

Walker was yanked from sleep, pushed past his mother, who was saying something about school the next day.

"You're always bitching at me to do something with him and now that I am you can just get the hell out of my way." In a sense, his mother must have died, Walker thinks, just like his father. But his father hadn't died, had only disappeared. Still, he and his brother were real orphans. She gave up, something she usually didn't do. He saw her face as he looked back. She was standing in the doorway. She turned the porch light on. Maybe she thought it might be the last time she'll see either one of them and she wanted to see them clearly, or maybe she'd done it out of old habit, to simply light their way safely down the dark sidewalk and leave a light for them to find their way home again.

Whatever was happening, it might be worth his mother's defeat. He's in a privileged situation, even if it didn't begin the way he would have liked. He doesn't dare question it. He grips the seat in front of him and holds on for dear life.

His own small face enters the mirror behind his brother's as he kneels on the backseat and leans forward. His elbows rest on the front seat like in church at the communion rail. The altar he faces, that dims down so quickly after a car passes, is the dashboard, the shrine of his brother's new freedom. The aquarium green dials of the Chevy, the speedometer straight up at sixty, the gas gauge three-quarters full, the temperature just above the middle ground between hot and cold, all of these things measure the increments of freedom. He knows it has been bought on credit, that there's something iffy about keeping it. He knows in advance Lee will never let him drive it. The odometer rolls slowly. Right before his eyes three nines change to zeroes and he watches a one appear in the slot to the left where no number has ever been before.

He can't think of anything to say; he wonders if he can speak. All he knows is that it doesn't seem right to talk, to break the strange spell that has come upon his brother.

They are crossing into Florida. He sees the sign that welcomes them and imagines it has been put up just for their arrival. The motion of the car gradually eases him and he allows himself to look forward, just a little, to Cape Canaveral. For weeks he's been thinking about nothing else but this rocket launch. He never dreamed he'd actually be going. His room is plastered with pictures of rockets, a map of the universe, and best of all, glow-in-the-dark stars and planets he's pasted carefully on the ceiling. The first night he turned off the light the stars in the ceiling jumped, or so it seemed. He was that startled by the beauty and suddenness of their appearance, so unlike the gradual brightening in the real night sky. He stayed awake until whatever light the phosphorescence had captured slowly faded, which was long before dawn. Still, he'd had a sense of the universe letting him in for a look. The room that had always been a small refuge from the storm that constantly raged between his mother and brother suddenly became an infinite place, no longer hemmed in by four walls, a ceiling, and a floor. It suddenly had dimension, majesty.

It made the room deeper, higher. It barely contained him anymore. In the dark he soared.

Now they race toward the countdown. When dawn breaks, they will be standing on a sand dune in Florida by the Atlantic Ocean watching a rocket leave the earth, defy gravity, lift its earthly weight heavenward. It's as if the universe, until now, has excluded mankind and is now about to repeal some law and let him in.

He must have slept again because his brother's hand shakes him awake. "We're here, but we have to hurry," he says. Walker crawls out of the back seat and finds himself in a parking lot with hundreds of cars. They join a ragged procession of people trudging up a dune. The beach grass is sharp and scratches his bare feet. He's embarrassed to realize he's still in his pajamas, that his brother had not thought to bring along any clothes or shoes for him. And they're cowboy pajamas, which seem stupid and babyish here. His brother's long strides are hard to keep up with and for a moment he is afraid he will be left behind. How will his brother ever find him again? Lee looks so determined to get to the top of the hill, he doesn't have room for any other thoughts; he doesn't even seem to know Walker is with him.

When they finally crest the dune Walker's out of breath. One foot was cut by a piece of glass that stuck up through the sand. He limps up to where his brother, hands on hips, feet apart, lays claim to the very spot on which he stands. A king surveying his rightful kingdom. Walker looks down the hill and immediately forgets the pain in his foot. The scene that stretches out below is overwhelming, like something on the scale of the pictures in his brother's dog-eared history books on ancient civilizations: the throngs of people, complicated scaffolding, a pointed thing rising up. Behind it, the Atlantic Ocean, brightening from gray to blue as the sun begins to burn through the haze at the horizon. A thread of what looks like steam boils from the bottom of the rocket as if it's simmering. The rocket is barely held back by the cranes around it—a bronco inside a chute just before it's released. They wait and the waiting is almost more than he can stand. It's going to happen, any minute now. They did not come all this way for nothing.

From out of nowhere he hears the word "nine" taken up by the crowd. Then eight. Each number louder than the one before as more people hear the countdown and join in, a congregation in unison, a calibrated prayer.

At three the rocket flares. Then there are no numbers left to count, only the enormous explosion, the shuddering of the rocket in its cradle, the terrible effort it takes to rise. The scaffolding parts like a pair of giant upended calipers. Everything is in slow motion, and the rocket, freed from its metal harness clears the last thing that holds it and rises straight up, a heated white cloud blasting beneath it. Walker stands on his toes as if that will help. Something in him feels afraid it will teeter, that everything will fall. It continues upward though it does wobble, once. He watches until he can't see it anymore. Some people have binoculars, one man has a telescope. He can see these things as he brings his eyes back to earth, but what he begins to hear, louder now than the roar of the rocket is the cheering of the crowd. Hats are thrown in the air, children held up on their brothers' shoulders and even the grownups jump up and down. His own brother stretches upward, arms raised, head thrown back, shouting, "Yes! Yes!" Walker senses the freedom in all of it. He doesn't understand exactly why his brother is so moved, only that he is. Walker has never felt more amazed, or more alone. But for a moment, on a bright morning on a sandy hill in Florida, he sees his older brother become a grateful man.

Walker feels a love so sharp and clear it cuts away the anger that has always surrounded it. What he remembers now upon waking is not the spectacle of the rocket, but the beauty of his brother, lifted and in awe, beyond earthly despair.

The wind hasn't lessened a bit. The place is utterly still except for the woman's voice and the wind, which has lessened, but only slightly. He hears a man say, "It's comin' in at 8:04."

Other voices come through the wind. He turns to watch the first wave of people come to the fence, stake their positions. A blond child wrapped in a pink blanket trails it behind her like a winding sheet. A man pushes another man in a wheelchair. Walker watches them come. They seem to be coming right at him but hardly look at him when they pass by and line up along the fence. He could be a ghost without a body or a voice. He's that transparent.

"Six minutes," someone says, and the word ripples down the line.

The thought comes, which has been waiting in the wings for this moment. *I wish Lee was here to see this.* The spectacle, the thrill, being in on something historic. He'd love it.

"They changed the runway because of the wind," a man next to Walker says. He lifts a pair of binoculars to his face. "It's a good half mile from here—we'll barely be able to see it."

"No!" Walker shouts. He's frightened at his voice, how angry it sounds. Lee's voice. The idea of it not being able to land is starting to mean that everything else, everything else in his entire life will come to nothing. If Truth is in the middle of a big mistake, has he already made it? Is there something more to lose? Hasn't he lost enough?

"There it is!" someone shouts and collectively the crowd turns its face into the sun. A silver, hurtling speck breaks the sound barrier with a boom that sounds like two trains colliding. For a moment Walker feels an excitement that seems to lift him, beyond all the hopelessness that's been passed to him.

The silver spacecraft comes down like an arrow pinpointed to Earth, and for a moment it takes his breath away. But when it touches down it's so far away that the exact moment of contact is lost. People with binoculars strain to keep it in their sights. The distant speck disappears from view, comes to a stop somewhere behind a row of sheet metal hangars.

It's over. The crowd stands for a moment, its shadow still thrown onto the runway, but shortening as the sun climbs higher. All that anticipation and it's over so fast. It could have been any plane landing. Nobody seems to know what to do. Some people still look up as if they expect any minute for the real spectacle to begin.

The crowd stays for a few moments, then people begin to turn, slowly fold up their chairs and blankets. They walk reluctantly away, heading toward the herd of vehicles perfectly parked and waiting their riders' return.

A lifetime of dominoes falling and now he's down to the last one. He feels it teetering, fighting to stay upright. He stands by himself on the deserted tarmac, watches the solid mass of the crowd leak away, moving faster toward the cars as if they suddenly can't wait a minute longer to get out of there. Walker thinks he sees a red and white Rambler station wagon, but he can't say for sure. He has an almost uncontrollable urge to run after it.

A commanding voice that began in a bullhorn wavers in a gust of wind. "Gates will be closed in ten minutes. Please clear the area."

The Mojave moves in on him, surrounds him. Remnants of old forest hang on to thin soil, trying not to be blown away. But he feels it. Sooner or later, even the most stubborn tree will want it, that bending, that giving in.

The truth is right outside the gates, waiting. All he sees beyond is the windblown tired desert, the scant, bent cottonwoods, and when he looks in the rearview mirror to see if someone's trying to catch up to him he sees nothing except his own frightened face.

And Lee. Not behind the wheel for once, but riding behind him. He's wearing cowboy pajamas, the gun on his lap, the chamber empty. Lee leans back. He lets his brother drive.

Stingamati

Dawn comes so red it does not look real. The men of the village stream down to the beach as they do every morning, not heeding the warning. Seventeen boats are hauled from their sheds down the black sand, twenty chanting men to each. This morning I see them as if for the first time—how small they look—the boats and the men like insects, a body with many wriggling legs. The sea so huge behind them. The boats have voices—they groan, singing a song of their own as they scrape across the rocks. They don't want to go to the sea today. But they clear the surf, and the men swing their paddles. I've seen all this hundreds of times before, but this time I see it clearly—how impossible the odds are, these little men in their little boats hunting for something as big as a whale.

I know their rituals by heart: the harpooner sprinkling holy water on the rope, the sharpening of the blades. A dozen heads bow in prayer. On each boat, someone stands to raise the palm sail. For a few minutes the rising sun catches in each of seventeen sails—the insects unfold their wings and change from things that creak and crawl into creatures that might at any minute fly, that might actually be able to catch a whale. They are powerful and beautiful as they round the point, then grow smaller and smaller until they become specks on the blue horizon, no more than a handful of commas on an enormous blank page.

I stopped going out on the boats to hunt for whale two years ago. Father van der Meer had asked me to work for him—assist him in the mass. I could not be a harpooner like my mother's father, stand on the *hamalolo* that juts out beyond the bow, balanced for hours, watching for the whale. The truth is, I'm afraid of the sea, of whales most of all. The way they dive and surge and fight when struck, the way they finally give themselves away.

The boats, the life of this village, that carry in each piece of wood the whole history of the ancestors, are no relations of mine. I wear a white shirt and dark blue trousers instead of a sarong. I carry a book instead of a knife or a harpoon. The men always stare at me when we pass on the path. I am not a man to them. I have no father and am known as the priest's pet. And the women—well, they never know what to make of me.

I watch from my hiding place behind the sheds until the boats become less than specks on the horizon. They spread out, weaving back and forth on the loom of the sea, hoping the ancestors will send them a whale for all their right-doing, and that the Christian God, if he is not busy elsewhere, might also answer their prayers.

I am waiting for the first radio to come to Lamalera. The Friday boat from Lewolebe clears the rocky point, dazzling white when the sun hits it, its smoke scribbling a long unintelligible word on the sky. People pour out of their houses when they hear the horn blast; we have all been waiting so long for this day.

A box marked "Sony" is lowered into the waiting sampan below, then brought ashore, and today Alo Bataona is the most important man on the island and the whole village follows him— more people than go to the church to hear Father van der Meer give Sunday mass or to listen to the *kepala desa* when he sits beneath the village tree to teach us to remember the *adat*, the old ways.

We are a noisy procession all the way to Alo's house. He takes the radio from its carton and places it in the open window so all can hear. He adjusts its position so that it sits exactly in the center; he places the batteries inside, almost tenderly. He prepares to turn the knob—his hand rests upon on it, but first he turns to us to delay the moment a few seconds longer so that it will be inscribed forever in our minds. These last few seconds of silence are so charged that it seems the radio will surely break apart from the strain of so much expectation. Even Alo's yellow dog named Yellow Dog, even the children—they are all waiting; the village has never been so quiet.

We have been hearing about it for months. We have seen pictures in a magazine but they have told us nothing. Alo has said it will be like hearing God himself, speaking, a noise beyond our imaginations. Everyone wonders—will he speak in Bahasa Indonesian, or some language exclusive to heaven?

At Sunday mass when I helped Father van der Meer with communion I looked beyond the heads of those bowing at the altar rail to the wall behind it with its painted cross and Jesus Christ hung upon it knowing that on the other side of that wall was the shrine I had made—without priests and commandments, sin and salvation—a faith in music, to make noise, joyful or otherwise. If there was a hell, it was silence. For a long time the only thing lacking to complete my religion was the voice of John Lennon. In my religion there is no waiting for a messiah, he is already among us. A writer of songs, a man with a dream. Any moment now he will sing.

A voice explodes from the radio and the children scream and run away. Yellow Dog barks wildly and the people pull back. The words are in English, which I alone understand. Father van der Meer taught me this language, but he is not among us this morning. I walk forward into the empty space. Everyone is watching me now. The man in the radio is saying something about John Lennon—that is how I know my prayers have been answered. I have been reading so much about him from the magazines that come to the mission library. I have torn out the pictures of him and put them on my wall in my room and now, his name from the radio, and then the voice itself, John Lennon's voice singing "Revolution" so loud and strong I cannot help it; I fall on my knees right there in the dirt.

The children are caught in the music and start jumping up and down like sand fleas and the dancing spreads until everyone is moving; churned-up dust rises like a great cloud around us. It is better than I hoped for; it is nothing like I'd imagined, and I've spent such a long time imagining. And best of all is the way the music is everywhere and Alo has only to touch the radio to make it louder.

I've read the Bible over and over. I thought I could crack the code of God, but there's nothing there for me. Father van der Meer took the mystery out of Jesus—someone who let himself be nailed to a piece of wood, who cried in front of everyone to a father who had clearly forgotten him. There's nothing new about that—fathers forgetting sons—it's the oldest story in the world. The real miracle of Jesus is that he didn't tear his hands away from the nails so he could shake his fists at God.

I don't know how to pray, who to pray to. Jesus seems far away, and the ancestors know my blood does not come entirely from them. My mother died when I was three years old, of malaria, and all I remember of her is the way her spine felt as she carried me, tied with a cloth strap to her back. The row of vertebrae, like stones pressing into my chest and stomach, left her mark on me forever. But it is better to have no father, for him to be a complete mystery. Even my mother didn't know. So he can be anyone, even John Lennon. After all, he has an Asian son.

Now I have something to believe in, something all my own. The children are dancing wild now. The song ends and I want another and another, and then the man is saying that he will be playing John Lennon's music all day and all night to honor him, and then he's saying, "John Lennon was shot and killed today in the streets of New York City."

What is he talking about? I say out loud, "NO!" this can't be, and the man is saying something about a man waiting with a gun. A man who said he was a fan. I cover my ears. I do not want to know his name. I start yelling and everyone is looking at me. No one understands a word of it. Then I see Father van der Meer, who understands all too well. In his blue eyes, a righteous satisfaction as if what he has predicted all along has just come to pass. It was he who told me to forget about John Lennon when he saw the pictures on my wall. He said that any man who had boasted that he was more popular than Jesus deserved to lose his voice since he'd already lost his soul. Father van der Meer looks at us all—his congregation, and to me in particular he gives one last look of pity before he walks away.

But as the next song comes, "Imagination," I know that Jesus was only half the story. It is not blasphemy that makes me say this, but faith: God found His true son singing and has just called him home.

When I get back to my room the door is open. The walls have been stripped bare and the place where I have read Shakespeare and the Bible and a songbook with all the Beatles lyrics an anthropologist from Oxford left behind is nothing more than the cell of a monk, bare and punishing. I sink down to my mat on the floor, stare at the empty walls. Gone are the photographs of John Lennon: Him with a cap and without one, with a beard or shaven clean, sitting in a bed with Yoko Ono, with the Maharishi in India, with Sergeant Pepper's Lonely Hearts Club Band. Standing at the edge of Strawberry Fields, looking through sunglasses with a T-shirt on that says "New York City," striding with the others across Abbey Road.

I feel a grief so deep that I don't know where to go, what to do. The picture I loved most of all, John Lennon with a baby in his arms—his son, Sean—with Yoko, is gone. He stopped singing for him so that he could learn to listen. And he'd just started singing again.

Now I believe this: the Christian God is a god who taketh away. He discovers what you most want and then he takes it from you. John Lennon is dead. I will never know my father. The two things seem terribly connected. My flawless grammar that I've worked so hard on leaves me and I want only to swear. I feel a stranger to the place I have been living for the last seventeen years.

I leave my room through the little door that goes into the back of the altar. The door opens onto the enormous vaulted ceiling, the high windows through which the eyes of stars look in. Candles flicker on the altar. I go to the piano—the one I've played every Sunday service since I was seven—stately hymns and solemn processions. I sit on the bench, push back the hinged cover over the keys. I rest my fingers on a C-major chord but I do not play. My fingers want only to crawl up the black keys and pound. And then they do. The sound is terrifying, not beautiful. I keep my foot on the pedal and all the notes run together. I am banging as if the instrument is a door that is locked to me. And then, I let up on the pedal and the notes let go of other notes and new ones come and I am climbing up the keyboard, shouting as I go, and I know I am getting somewhere that I might never get back from—not a place of punishment and humiliation, but a place that wants me. It is like I am playing my way up a ladder and at the top of it all the musicians are leaning down from their own country in heaven, reaching their hands toward me, calling and pulling me upward. I am rising, I am falling, I am inside music and it is playing me. I think I might be dying and I am not afraid to go.

Out of nowhere, behind me, a hand reaches out and pushes the cover down over the keys, over my hands. "How dare you? How dare you desecrate this holy place? You will never touch this instrument again. I did not give you music to be used this way." Father van der Meer stands there shaking, his face red with rage.

My fingers swollen, throbbing, but not broken, I turn around slowly, the words coming to me as I turn. "You did not give me music. The music was always in me."

Then I leave the church, back through the door behind the altar to my room. Father van der Meer follows me but I press myself against the door to keep him out. The handle on the door squeaks feebly once, then I hear his footsteps move heavily away.

I try to sleep, but sleep must not recognize the room anymore; I leave so it can find me.

Tonight I wander through the village, *stingamati,* a Lamaholot word that still rings of Portuguese: a wound. To us it means half-dead. Tonight I am *stingamati* while everyone else is dreaming.

I can't stop thinking about one of the pictures of John Lennon and Yoko Ono in a magazine a tourist left behind. In the picture he looks like he's just been born from her, that he is coming alive. The picture has always made me think of Mary Magdalen. I think Jesus went to her because he had second thoughts about going to heaven. He knew there's nowhere to turn, finally, but to a woman—the oldest darkness of all, where the body, becomes the sea again. Right now all I know for certain is I have to find her, my own Magdalena.

Magdalena is her Bible name, the one moved in front of whatever her Indonesian name had been. Father van der Meer named us, as if he were the father of us all. She never speaks, except to me. No one will kiss Magdalena because she has come in the world with a devil mark: her upper lip melted as if from a great heat inside the womb. The young boys always throw pebbles at her and chant "Magdalena Magdalena Magdalena." So she always seems to be walking to the rhythm of her name.

I used to watch Magdalena on the beach when she was ten years old. It was the last year she swam naked with the boys. She was not afraid like all the other girls of the water serpents—maybe she believed it was the mark upon her mouth that saved her, that all the harm that could be done had come all at once upon her while she was still in the womb and so could live the rest of her life free of fear.

But even though she went into the waves with the boys she never could go to sea with the men the way she wanted. Her father was a harpooner and every day except for Sunday she would watch him go. She used to stand there on the beach and wail, a large voice she was proud of, that came out strong in spite of the crooked mouth. Women are not allowed on the boats—it's bad luck for the hunt. Everyone believes this, but no one knows exactly why.

The first time I remember speaking to Magdalena she ran, dripping from the sea, her skin a polished bronze, her nipples flat as coins. It was one of those rare days when a whale came close enough to shore to see. The men had already brought in the boats for the afternoon, hauled them up the beach, and dragged them into the sheds. Pak Joe, who'd lost an arm to a shark, came running down the path, shouting, "Baleo! Baleo!" because he'd seen the whale sounding offshore from his house on the hill. Soon everyone was running to bring the boats out again. Magdalena's father was the first one at the boat sheds, and I watched her pleading with him to take her this one time. She had her fists clenched as she ran alongside the boat that was being dragged down the beach by twenty men, and for a moment I almost believed she would be lifted up, that she would have done what no other girl had simply because she asked. But her father spoke sharply to her and she stood as if slapped, and stayed on that spot after all the boats had left, her fists still closed tight. I walked slowly toward her and stood beside her looking where she was looking—out to sea where she could not go.

"Why?" she demanded of me because I was the only one there. I didn't know how to answer.

"Why," she continued, "do you do not go when you are able to?"

"Because," I found myself answering and I had never had this idea before, "because I am bad luck, too."

She reached her hand out to push against the front of my shorts. "You are no girl," she said, then took her hand away. I was so shocked I thought I would fall over.

"No," I managed to say. "I am no girl, but I am not that kind of man, either." I nodded toward the now distant boats. I looked at her body, at the little patches of black sand that stuck to her arms, her thrust-out chin, the great mass of tangled black hair, and the smooth, hairless place between her legs that would soon be covered up forever. She was alone, in the last days of a freedom no other girl in the village had cared enough to keep. I wanted her to keep fighting, to win, for both of us.

"That kind of man out there," she said, "is afraid."

"Of what?"

"Falling in the water because of a girl. And not just a pretty girl—an ugly girl could make it happen. My mother says it's because a woman has a mystery. She can turn a man's mind from God."

"Do you have it?" I asked.

She thought hard for a minute and her hands curled tight again with the effort. It was as if she were searching everywhere inside herself for it, something bright behind the bone.

"No," she said, opening her eyes again, relaxing her hands. "Not yet."

"When you do," I said, "will you show it to me?"

"You might fall."

I said it didn't matter, and when I think of it now, waiting by this path for her seven years later, I am amazed at what a little girl understood so well back then, that it first takes a fall before you can rise and get up and become a true man.

Magdalena's mystery is coming soon—I can feel it. Any minute now she will give it to me.

I wait in the shadow of a tree by the path listening for the steady soft slap of her feet coming back from market in Wulandoni. "Magdalena, Magdalena," I am chanting under my breath. "Magdalena, come to me."

What if she will not? The thought is too painful to think but now that I've thought it, it will not let go of me.

Magdalena's bare feet hardly make a sound. I don't hear her until she is almost on top of me—my breathing is that loud. She is coming toward me and she doesn't know I am waiting; she is coming toward me and I do not know what I will do.

The moon knows. It slips out of the clouds to see for itself. I think I have come to throw a pebble, but what flies from my hand is a stone. A stone taking its aim from anger, from need. It hits her shoulder and when I hear her cry out, I am no boy; I want the things that should belong to a man. The basket of rice she was balancing on her head falls and the pale, white grains go flying everywhere.

Magdalena stoops to pick up the stone, looks up into the sky as if God himself has finally joined the children who always mock her and cast his own verdict down. For a moment, there is only the sound of the sea below the cliff, rushing through the rocks, the muffled tolling of the mission bell.

Magdalena cries out. I step out from the shadows where I have been waiting. It isn't words of men I want to say to her but animal sounds—a groan, a growl, a great shuddering howl. I thrust my other hand between her legs but her sarong is wrapped tight as a bandage. I pull the cloth quickly, tearing it, until she is standing naked in front of me. She is not a child. Her body is flawless, she is a woman below her mouth. I touch that mouth with my hand and feel the cleft beneath my palm—softer than I imagined it would be.

Magdalena's face, inches from mine, her mouth covered, blood seeping through the cracks between my fingers. My blood. Her eyes so wild, her teeth surprisingly sharp. How perfect. She bit me.

I wake, if that's what you can call it, on the beach behind one of the boat sheds with no memory of how I got here. The boats have already gone out to sea for the day. I have slept like someone dead, wakened by a sound. Crazy Anna. Her white hair flies as she tosses her head and wails, calling to the souls of the dead. But why is she here? I look down at my hand, the half moon marks of teeth. Then I remember. We climbed inside one of the boats and struggled there, crying and shouting until we both surrendered.

Stingamati. My body is weightless now. My mind a white moth pulled between one dream and another, unable to tell which one is waking. Everyone is looking out to sea. At first I think someone has seen a whale blowing offshore or a tourist boat coming with people who have money to buy ikat and carvings. But there is no tourist boat, no whale, and when I turn to check the angle of the sun behind me, already behind the mountain, I know how late it is. Only fourteen of the seventeen boats are coming back. Everyone watches for those last three specks on the horizon. After a while, they sit down in the sand to wait. The children wait. Even Yellow Dog rests on his paws. I see no sign of Magdalena.

The dark takes a long time to come. Everyone lights whale oil lanterns and the *kepala desa* himself comes to light a fire. It twists in the breeze like a red tongue trying to speak.

One thing is becoming clear: the ancestors are dreaming this. They are dreaming everything, including me, making a story and a lesson so perfect the Christian God Himself surely must envy the genius of it and be sorry He didn't dream of it first.

I want to leave but cannot move. I sink back down behind a pile of rope. No one looks in my direction. Their attention belongs to the sea, the awful quiet of it except for the few waves that break the silence, that fume around the rocky point. The moon is no help. It's low and muddy yellow, fat with secrets it won't give away. Shadows rush across the sand. Even the stars when they come are mixed up in clouds. On the hill behind the town, the mission bell begins to ring and does not stop. Father van der Meer, pulls on the rope until his palms bleed, calling out to God, who once again is not listening.

Stingamati. My spirit escapes, flies over the sea but is soon tied to the men on the missing boats. I sail straight into their story with them, the story that is becoming mine. The hole that has always been my life is opening—I can feel it gaping—as if I am tied to them and every inch of ocean that widens between us is making room. This is my punishment, my lesson. To see, to hear, to feel it all and not be able to do a thing. I am falling now, falling all the way in.

Three boats, tied together in a long line, and out in front, the whale, a gray mountain, rising. Wounded. Furious. She drags them behind her, farther and farther out to sea.

Five harpoons in her. Bad throws, all of them, none near enough to her heart to kill her, but deep enough to bear the weight of three boats and thirty-five men. How long before she gives up, they wonder. They will wait. I watch helplessly, and I know what they do not: this is no ordinary whale. This one is inhabited, filled with the spirits of the ancestors who whisper to her what must be done: "Teach them a lesson," they are chanting, a lesson that will never be forgotten, that will be told again and again. A story more powerful than Jesus and the crucifixion, more final than John Lennon's murderer waiting with a gun.

The whale dives deep, and for a few minutes it seems she has stopped, died at last below them. The boats sit there and the water is flat and still. But I can feel the water roll before they do, and suddenly she breaks the surface, shoots upward, aiming her body at the thing that hurts her. She thrashes her fluke just once with a stroke so powerful it breaks one of the boats. Shouts from the men as the water rushes in. Oars like sticks float away, the water jug bobbing, tobacco baskets spinning as they disappear. The boat is broken, but does not sink. Still, the men leave it to swim to the second boat. Then the water is quiet again.

The whale waits far below. But soon the ancestors urge her upward again. "Show them, show them," they whisper. I can hear them perfectly. They are angry, they will be satisfied; they will claim their power again. The second boat cracks as if it's a tree struck by lightning and ten men leap into the water, then swim frantically toward the last boat. The same boat Magdalena and I lay together in. They all get in and the boat rides low in the water, weighed down with all of them. The whale disappears after sounding, gives them time to argue, to break all the laws by which they hunt and live: to never speak in anger of the whale, to never have disagreements on the boat—these things always bring bad luck and are strictly forbidden. But they are frightened and fight over what to do. The young men shout not to cut the ropes, that the whale will give herself up. The oldest man says very quietly that the spirits are inside of her and will never let go.

The whale decides. She arches her body again, throws herself against the boat, but in her cleverness, does not break it completely. I feel her doubling back, coming toward them again. The oldest man saws at the rope with shaking hands. "Hurry!" I scream, but my mouth doesn't even open. The whale turns at the last instant though she thrashes her fluke one last time as if to slap the boat, almost gently this time, a little reprimand. Still, she breaks off the harpooner's bridge as if it's nothing more than a stick. She dives below and does not rise again.

The men sit, wet and shivering in the wind that comes out of nowhere. Someone has a smoke and passes it around. The dawn is far away, they've run out of drinking water. There is no food. They begin to cry.

I beg for deafness, and yet, I can't stop myself from listening. The ancestors have made me an ear into which they pour this one endless story I will hear for the rest of my life. The men are making up a song, they are singing, "Tears flowing, tears flowing, I paddle my boat, my tears flowing." I am listening, but I cannot sing.

A storm fills up what's left of the night and the men open their mouths to rain. They gnaw on pieces of wet, soft wood as if they're pieces of bread. I am afraid they will devour the boat, that the very thing that keeps them from drowning will soon be gone.

The whale swims west, the five harpoons like quills still deep inside her. She bleeds a trail behind.

Stingamati. My body is pulled back to the beach on the tide of this waking dream. I can do nothing but listen to the wailing and praying of the people; each sound pins me deeper inside my body. All I know for certain is this pain in my left hand. There's water in a wooden jug, water so old it tastes like poison, bitter as the wood that holds it. Maybe it's something in the water, or the lack of food, or the constant tolling of the bell, but I live inside a trance. So this is purgatory, I think, still alive just beyond the living. Listening, smelling, seeing what you can no longer have.

I peek over the hull. The moon looks on—a monocle, a pearl-colored lens on a black, black sky. There is a new sound now, coming down the hill toward the beach. An unintelligible sound. I run my fingers over the wound in my hand.

The first thing I see is Father van der Meer coming down from the church, a lantern swinging in his hand. But he never comes out at night. He told me once he's been afraid of the dark since he was a child, that the fear never left him, so it must be something very important happening to bring him out of his house. His swollen knees I rub lineament onto every night after dinner bend painfully, I can tell, at every one of fifty-two stone steps hacked into the hill. He moves slowly, reluctantly, like someone descending into hell. At the bottom of the hill, a crowd of people starts to gather, waiting. The *kepala desa* himself watches, as if calculating how long it will take for Christian authority to arrive.

Magdalena is coming down to the beach now, heading straight for the *kepala desa.* Her mouth is closed. She holds out her hand and opens it. On her naked, upturned palm, the stone. Before the priest reaches the bottom, the *kepala desa* holds out something for everyone to see. I hear the words: "The stone will tell us, the stone will have its say."

Father van der Meer reaches the last step. His robes look slack and dark in the flickering light. His eyes scan the crowd and come to rest on the *kepala desa* and their eyes meet: open and terribly calm. The *kepala desa* slowly closes his hand around the stone.

Phosphorescence shimmers in the breaking waves, green ghosts dancing. I can't stand up. I crawl into the circle of firelight by the fire. At first, the *kepala desa* is the only person who notices me. He sits so straight and strong he looks more like a tree than a man, something so deeply rooted he can hold his own against monsoon wind. Magdalena steps out of the shadows behind him. The *kepala desa* doesn't speak; he doesn't have to. He gives the stone to Magdalena. Magdalena comes to me.

I reach toward her, palm open. Her fist opens. A gray, unremarkable rock. Such a small thing to have caused so much. When she drops it in my palm I expect it to be heavy, but instead it feels almost hollow, as if the center has been sucked out of it. I know, as the wailing stops, as the people slowly turn: the stone in my hand is only something that stands for stone. I put it in my mouth but cannot swallow or spit it out. It hangs inside me, a clapper in a hollow bell, ringing.

The fire before me flickers. Everyone is listening. Magdalena takes the stone from my mouth. I tell them what they want to know.

Rain and tears, rain and tears. Out of the darkness a light comes, an eye looking right at the men in their broken boat as they are preparing to die. Tall masts and an orchestra, people dancing in long dresses on deck. The men must think they have died and are sailing right into English heaven. The future keeps coming toward them, nearly runs over them as they cry out, "*Tolong! Tolong!* Help us!"—small sounds against the orchestra. But the eye sees them and circles around throwing light all over them. Everyone comes to the railing to watch. That's when I see myself—not inside the sinking boat with the men, not on the beach with the people of the village, but leaning over the railing—a young man in a John Lennon T-shirt and a pair of blue denim jeans. From the railing, I see what the tourists on the ship see. We are looking down a long tunnel that narrows down to this—a shimmering, moving image so old it is farther back in time than our imaginations will take us.

Shivering, skinny crying men in a broken boat looking, not into a past they can't remember, but toward a future they can't even imagine. It's the end of the world," someone says. And I think, "So this is how it ends."

But there's more.

The men are lifted up. They must have climbed a ladder, but in my story I see them rising, lighter than air because they've cried so many tears. They rise out of the broken wooden boat into the sleek fiberglass hull of the future. Someone has a video camera. Someone always does. The men are wrapped in blankets, given hot soup, and the rain drips off them, a drop at a time onto the floor, flowing past the high heels and hundred-dollar shoes.

I stop. I cannot say any more. I do not see any more. The eye that was in me has closed.

"Where are our boats?" the people cry, as if the boats are our grandfathers, and without them we have no story of ourselves.

"At the bottom of the sea," I say.

And the mourning begins all over again.

I come to the empty boat shed almost every night now. For me, it is a holy place, the only place where I can think, or dream, or try to pray. Heavy yellow light spills from the blackened lamp that hangs in the rafters when I light the wick. The wick draws up the oil of the whale, the last one that freely gave itself without a fight, the one who came to feed us, not to teach us anything.

Tonight, the small light shines on this: a wooden plank raised over the black sand and, resting upon it like bones of the ancestors, two pieces of wood. Not the boat, but what stands for a boat. A bowl from which a people can be stirred and born. The boats aren't coming back, the vigil is over—but I keep looking. For what? I don't even know anymore. I am left with the light, the beautiful, ancient light, to which nothing will return.

I will not sleep tonight. Sometimes I think I will never sleep again. There will only be this story winding back on itself, endlessly repeating, changing a little each time. The lamp in the boat shed falters. In a year or so, the oil will be replaced by kerosene, bought, not bartered, with money changing hands. Nothing on this island will ever be the same. The story will keep telling itself, and I will become a part of history—more talked about here than Alo and his radio, more famous than either God or John Lennon, and, like Judas to Jesus, necessary.

Since I am no longer given waking dreams, I make my own. I dream of myself, the way I would look leaning over the railing of the tourist ship watching the men of our village pulled aboard. And then? And then?

Then I will sail to America wearing a John Lennon T-shirt and blue denim jeans. I will walk from the pier to the Dakota. I will stand on the place where he fell. I will have headphones on, but they will not completely shut out the noise coming through an open window interrupting my ritual. I have brought a candle with me. It will not light. I look up. I see a face in a window high up. Yoko Ono, I'm sure. Across the street in the park, a game of baseball. Everyone groans in the strikeouts, hollers in the home runs. What is this most sacred of American rituals? I cannot see it, the diamond or what it means, the small stitched ball soaring when it is hit hard, the men in no danger running, running for their lives.

Almost Egypt

To the People of the Future from Maud Farrell

Monte Ne, Arkansas
July 5, 1929

I saw it only once, just the other night in a dream: Coin Harvey's pyramid rising from these Ozark Mountains like he said it would, the only thing left of mankind still standing tall through the ruins of time. In the dream there was a door at the top of the pyramid and inscribed upon a metal plate his own words, *When this can be read go below and you will find records of the cause and death of a former civilization.* He told us of the three doors, one below the other. He said he didn't know how far the pyramid would be covered up by a war or by just the Ozarks falling down on their own. He called it a caution "against the unpredictability of geology and the rampant greed of willful progress gone riot," a lot of words to say to mean he didn't trust nature or people as far as he could throw them.

In my dream the worst must have already happened because here I am at the last door wanting to see what he's put inside, impatient to read the book he's placed in the vault telling how we fell from grace by our hand and a great list of what not to do so it won't happen again. My hand floats toward the door but it's just out of reach, then it's gone—the door, the pyramid, the dream, the treasure of the future. I didn't act quick enough. In dreams I always feel like I'm a baby in my body, a baby with a great big mind that can barely move. But a voice followed me from the dream, floated above my bed. Mr. Harvey's voice, I'm sure of it, saying, "You have failed but your cries took the form of wings and were heard." What on earth did he mean?

I knew I had to tell Mr. Harvey to hurry. There's less time than he thought until the end of the world. It's breathing right down our necks. The pyramid will have to be built. *Soon.* But the 4th of July is right around the corner and everyone here at Monte Ne is getting ready for the fireworks, a dance, fiddle and flagpole-climbing contests. The pyramid is nothing more than gray lines scribbled on paper, the base it will sit on only a slab of Portland cement, its radio transmitter not here but only on order from the Philco Company that should be sending out the signal he promises will join all nations in peace and good will.

He's trying to get ready but he's too slow. I follow him late at night when he walks down Oklahoma Row with a lantern long after Monte Ne is asleep. I've seen him carrying things to put in a secret room under the amphitheater, all the things the pyramid will hold that say something about us—who we were. What we made. How we were so busy we forgot to keep our word.

Mr. Harvey slides a stone away near the base where the pyramid is to be built and disappears down a stairway into the earth. I follow him on tiptoe and hide myself in the crowded vault beneath the ground. There are shelves and shelves, and upon them, a great accumulation. Things have been disappearing from the hotel and he's driving the cooks and the head housekeeper mad. And here it all is together: A grandfather clock. A Singer sewing machine. A Victrola. A collection of marbles in a glass box. A dictionary. A cash register. A bathtub. A banjo. A zither. A printing press. A model of a flying machine. An hour glass. A brand-new suit on a hanger. A woman's fancy hat in a round box. A hammer. An egg beater. An appaloosa rocking horse with a leather saddle and a real tail and mane. I watch him, hidden in a cabinet between two velvet dresses and a medical mannequin that shows the river of blood through the body's veins. He runs his hand over the Singer sewing machine as if he loves the shape of it. He turns its wheel and I swear he sighs like a man in love at the beauty of how it works. He's becoming so distracted by all of these things that he doesn't want to part with any of it. And this from a man who wanted free silver and the end of usury. Maybe he knows he'll be forced to choose. Maybe he's afraid to offend the many wonderful things he'll have to leave behind. There's only room for so much, even in the future.

He doesn't know that I know about his secret room. He always left a few coins for me on the dresser when I cleaned his room. One time he also left the key, as if he wanted me to have it. As if he needed someone to share his secret with. I don't think he's actually *seen* me, doesn't know that I sit in the front of the amphitheater when he speaks there, doesn't know that I'm his best employee, that I have taken everything he says on faith. He read aloud from his book, because he was, at heart, a teacher to everyone, "The men and women have made a failure of this world. All now depends on you. You young people have a desire to have things right and good. You have sentiment and love of happiness. Your minds are not yet warped by the evil example that is being placed before you. It's up to you to take hold of this world, this disrupted civilization, and set it right; and as you grow older you will be stronger, you will create health and happiness, you will know the stars, the universe, and have eternal life!"

I don't know about eternal life. I just want to be *inside* the pyramid, to sleep until the future comes, to tell the first person to open the door that Mr. Harvey is a man of vision, ahead of his time, and that I, too, have a few things to say about what should not be repeated if the world is to be a better place. People of the future, I was an orphan on a train. I have no family and so I have no past. It disappeared in a heartbeat. And so when Mr. Harvey wants a place to put the truth, to save it for future times, he worries me. There's something I'm supposed to do right now to help him and I'm not sure what it is. I'm afraid there isn't enough time.

But before I do anything about the future I have to polish the floor in the great ballroom for the dance that will take place tonight. When I walk into the room Mr. Harvey is standing by the window looking out at the lake, his hands clasped behind his back. He almost looks like a prisoner in cuffs. But he unclasps his hands, turns, and catches me watching. He points out the window. "Come here, young lady, and tell me what you see." I put the polishing rag and the bucket on the floor and come to him. I look out the window that I had just washed the day before. I had done a good job—that's what I see at first. Then, when I look beyond the glass, it's like looking at a painting. There are boats upon the lagoon and the gondola brought all the way from Venice floats like a black swan through the arches of a stone bridge. There are women in pink parasols walking along the banks with children who laugh and splash in the clear water, getting their mothers' dresses wet. There are men in the boats, their coats draped over the seats, their white shirts rolled at the sleeves, their suspenders looking like harnesses making big X's across their backs as they row. I know Mr. Harvey didn't ask me to describe these things. It's more like he's asking me to say what's missing. So I say, "That's all very nice. But the pyramid, Mr. Harvey. I don't see the pyramid anywhere."

He looks completely taken aback. He looks right at me as if I'm more than just the hired help, as if I've whispered from the future to reprimand him. Since I have his attention I say, "I'd hurry if I were you."

I go back to my polishing. I concentrate on the piece of the floor in front of me, the grain in the wood rising from the dirt of the last dance a week ago. Mr. Harvey leaves the window abruptly and hurries out the door.

I'm thinking it would be better to try to reach the next civilization early when the people still believe the wheel is a great wonder, when they look up at the pyramid as a thing of mystery, before they figure out how to blow it up. But he didn't ask me my opinion. I'd said enough as it was.

I move across the floor on my hands and knees erasing the footprints Mr. Harvey left behind. He'd been experimenting with cement again, and he's always a little gray with the dust of it. He's one of those men that need a great deal of cleaning up afterward. He has extraordinarily big feet for not such a very tall man. There must have been a loose nail in his left boot because there's tiny half moon marks like a baby's fingernail everywhere he's been.

I give up trying to polish them halfway across the floor. I take my shoes off. I stand up, hike up my skirts, and step out, my left foot over his, then the right. He has a very long stride. I'm following his footsteps into the future, covering our tracks so we can disappear.

Out of the corner of my eye I see him pass by the door. Has he been watching? He stops, backs up, stands still in the doorway. He holds an electric fan in his arms. I've admired it often, how heavy it is sitting on the pedestal in the lobby. But since we have no electricity in Monte Ne we can only imagine the wind it would make. We better hurry with the electricity. People traveling want air-cooled rooms these days. They don't trust the mountain breezes to be enough any more.

In Mr. Harvey's arms its black blades turn a little as if he's been running; its cord dangles from the base like a long tail as if it pulls its power directly from him. Is it my imagination, or does he bow? He looks like an ambassador from the past presenting a gift, this beautiful, useless machine to move the air, whirl it into wind. He trips on the cord as he steps away, then he practically runs.

I can't explain it. I've had no feeling like it before and I've been around for seventeen years. I feel, in this moment, like a woman. Not a girl anymore. A woman with a certain power of my own, to quicken a man, or turn him to stone.

I run after him, calling out, "Wait, Mr. Harvey! It's me!" But it isn't me any more. He's running away, the cord flying behind him,

down the stairs, across the bridge, out of sight. And what did Mr.
Harvey see? It's the future he's running from. The future of me.

    Tonight the people come on the train from Rogers and
Fayetteville to see the fireworks, to dance to the band, the Black
Diamond Boys, from Bentonville. I watch it all from the wings
crowded with the kitchen staff. We laugh to see the fat man from
Cave Springs trying to shinny up the greased flagpole to get the
five-dollar bill taped on top, slipping back two feet for every foot
up. A boy who plays the fiddle catches my eye. His name is Kelly
Stilley from Harrison. And if the world is going to end then I'm
not going to waste any more time; I'm going to fall in love while I
still have half a chance.

    I listen to him play his songs for the contest, the required
"Arkansas Traveler" wild and fast as if the devil is chasing him but
he's far ahead and not a bit out of breath. Then he plays his own
composition and he files the strings so sweet with a bow he holds
light as a willow switch and the rosin powder falls on his shoulder
soft as snow.

    Mr. Harvey is out there in the audience of men judging the
contest. They don't allow women because it's too much of a dis-
traction or maybe they just want to smoke and drink to their heart's
content, at least for a little while. Not that I care about that. But I
have an idea as Kelly takes a bow that I could be the one to bring
the blue ribbon to him. He's going to win. He's that good. And
then he will see me.

    And he does win. So I'm ready. I grab the ribbon from the mas-
ter of ceremonies before he even knows what's happening and get
myself out there on the stage.

    He doesn't even look at me. He grabs the ribbon and goes. I
felt the barest brush of his hand. Now it's just me looking out into
that great room filled with blue smoke curling from cigars and the
tiny lights on the tables flickering through the long-stemmed

glasses filled to the brim with bubbling champagne. I can't help but think of the *Titanic,* how those people were sailing along celebrating and there was an iceberg with their name on it and only this time Mr. Harvey and I know what's out there somewhere ahead in the dark.

I can just make him out at the first table, lifting his glass to his lips. There's only silence. I turn to the audience, to Mr. Harvey in particular. A few point at me, laughing, as if I'm some kind of joke or one of the clowns outside with the children who's stumbled by accident onto the stage. But I'm not laughing. Glasses stop clinking and even the waiters stand still. Mr. Harvey himself leans forward, his arms on the white tablecloth, his hands folded like a preacher or the president. He's listening. Listening to *me.* To what I have to say.

"What's she doing up there?" someone finally says, loud from the back of the room.

So I go ahead and say it. "This is the future, Mr. Harvey," I say. "Right here."

Everyone looks at Mr. Harvey. He rises up slowly from his chair—you can hear it scrape on the floor as he pushes it back. A glass of champagne like half of an hourglass tips over, spilling toward the edge. I can hear it dripping on his shoes. He doesn't even look down at the mess he's made. Tomorrow I'll probably have to clean it up. He's looking at me. But then he takes the glass that fell over. Light catches it as he raises it up, a beautiful piece of etched crystal, to me. There isn't anything left in it except a drop but he drinks it anyway. And then a few people began to applaud, not sure if they should. The band starts up again.

The doors open and a great wave of women come in who've been waiting to find their husbands and dance. Mr. Harvey leaves the room, taking the glass with him. He wipes his forehead with a napkin, nearly knocking over a waiter as he bolts out the door.

I hurry off the stage and follow him. Mr. Harvey walks down to the water, to the empty amphitheater. A singing party on the gondola drifts at the far end of the lagoon. He stands there, looking out upon the water, then at the mausoleum beneath the trees where his only son, William, is buried, where he's left a place for himself next to him. I stand near him. We look toward the place where the pyramid will be. He can almost see it—he's drawn it so often. I can almost see it, the way it appeared complete and perfect in my dream. And I know there won't be enough room in it to hold the truth of who we were, at least not for very long.

He's still holding the glass. He sets it down on a stone bench. He bends to pick up something from the shore then pulls his arm back, then lets fly. I hear the stone skip—I count three. I find a stone of my own and throw it. Five.

Above us the sky breaks open and fireworks spray green and blue and red across the black sky as if streaks of heaven show through from the other side. It's beautiful—the bright explosions, the waltzes coming from the open windows of the hotel, the laughter of the people dancing who have all the time in the world.

People of the future, here we are: a plain man in a black-tailed coat standing on the edge of the water and a girl lifting up her skirts, wading in. We don't have to bring anything, do we? For now, the warm wind's miracle enough. The truth is, maybe the pyramid will never be built. To have thought of it will suffice. Can you feel it—the heat of our imagination, blowing through your hair? Will it be enough?

Note: Quotes from Mr. Harvey in "Almost Egypt" are from Coin Harvey's book, *Paul's School of Statesmanship* (Monte Ne, Ark.: 1936).

Riders on the Orphan Train

They stood in a long row on the platform at Pennsylvania Station, so alike in dark little coats. Blackbirds on a wire, Ezra thought. All of a feather, but we do not fly. Each held a cardboard suitcase with his or her name written on the side in ink, and due to the early morning drizzle on that September morning, some of the names were already blurred, the letters dripping into illegible graffiti. Ezra saw his own name changing shape in front of his face and it seemed the predictions of the people at the orphanage were already coming true—they wouldn't be needing those names, at least the surnames, much longer.

Ezra took a handkerchief out of his pocket and unfolded it carefully. They had been issued one each, along with a Bible and a new suit of clothes after a bath last night. He blotted the wet cardboard. Ezra Duvall—smudged, but legible. He folded the handkerchief again.

Inside the suitcase, a shirt, a pair of socks. A penny box of matches. A notebook, blank. Tucked between the pages, a thin piece of yellow paper on which was written his father's name and address. As soon as he got where he was going he would send a letter, let him know where to find him, and wait there until he came. The train rolled heavily, reluctantly, it seemed to Ezra, into the station, steam gusting from its dark stack. It looked like a creature breathing in winter air, though it was hot, sweltering eighty-five degrees. Indian summer, people were calling it. As if Indians had their own version of a season but had to wait for the other one to be over before theirs could begin.

The straight line of children broke apart even though Reverend

Horton and his assistant Mrs. Worthington did their best to keep them together. They'd stood long enough—they simply couldn't be still any more. Too much waiting: for the bath, the Bible, the suit of new clothes, and now the train, which was late to take them to their new homes out West where kind strangers would take them in.

The train shuddered to a complete stop. Conductors swung down from steps between cars like monkeys from trees Ezra had seen on his one trip to the zoo. This image occupied his mind for a moment, kept it from seizing up with the thought he had been trying not to think: We are leaving. We are leaving and we are never coming back. At least not any time soon.

"They finally found a way to be rid of you lot," Irish Danny had said last night. He shoveled coal in the basement at the orphanage, and had been working overtime—all that water to be heated for all those baths. "Very convenient," he'd said to Ezra, who stood near the open furnace door. "Free labor shipping out on the orphan train." Ezra had only come to bring him his dinner on a tray and had ended up having to listen to Danny's diatribe about a Protestant conspiracy to kidnap Catholic children and have them raised as Baptists or Lutherans in some Godforsaken western town. Ezra didn't want to listen, but the whole spectacle of Irish Danny heaving coal into a fiery furnace, shouting out his theories, was like getting a peek into purgatory and still being able to ascend the stairs back to the world.

Reverend Horton had stood at the head of the dining room, the new electric lamps along the wall emitting a steady, benevolent light, and explained to them that the train would stop in towns that had already been selected. People who had been deemed suitable through interviews conducted by local representatives of the Children's Aid Society of New York would be awaiting their arrival, which would be announced in the local newspapers. These people would, he said, be grateful for a chance to choose a child to help them on their farms or in their businesses. "You will all have homes! You will receive an education. You will become a part of a family where hard work and decency prevail!" He'd been so moved by the sight of them all listening, by the sound of a few of the older children crying, that he himself was moved to tears. But he'd mistaken the tears of the children for gratitude, as an affirmation of his mission. Later, Ezra heard crying again after lights out, and a boy two beds down was on his knees, not praying as Ezra had first assumed when he'd raised up on one elbow to see what he could from the dim light of the street lamp outside the curtained window. The boy was scratching his initials with a fork into the wooden headboard of his bed like a small ghost risen from a grave to carve its name in the unmarked stone.

The train waited, huffing in the station, the terrible banshee screech of its brakes at last died down. The line of children broke apart again as they moved toward the step the conductor had just set beneath the one that was too high for the littlest ones. The cardboard suitcases thudded against the step, the contents of some rattling as the children were helped up, one at a time. Even Lars, otherwise known as the bully boy, a tall Norwegian older than the rest, did what he was told, though he had swaggered last night down the rows of beds saying nobody was sending him anywhere he didn't want to go, that he had decided already he was going to Texas—out West—where his new family would give him a horse of his own. Now he lurched up the step, refusing the conductor's hand, but Ezra thought he looked just plain scared like everybody else. When Ezra climbed on and entered the car he was almost relieved to see Lars pushing another boy out of a seat next to a window he decided he had to have. At least some things didn't change.

Ezra deliberately sat in the back of the car on a seat only big enough for one. He wasn't an orphan. He still had a father. And although he wouldn't go so far as to say this whole thing was a mistake, he did feel it was temporary. He had come to the orphanage, delivered by an uncle who had enlisted in the army and was shipping out for Europe. Ezra had managed to get a look at his file when his uncle left the room with the Reverend to speak in the hall in private. "Mother, deceased," the file said, "sixteenth of July nineteen hundred and twelve." "Father's occupation: itinerant railroad worker." Itinerant, but alive. There had been a piece of paper with his father's name and the address where he worked. Ezra took it and hid it in his pocket. "Gerald Duvall, c/o The Pennsylvania Railroad, Philadelphia, Pennsylvania," it said. His uncle had been telling him for the two years since his mother died that his father would come back when he was "set up somewhere." His uncle couldn't wait anymore. The rooming house in Hell's Kitchen near Ninth Avenue had hardly been a home, though Ezra had slept there and had eaten mostly regularly and gone to school off and on while his uncle worked at the docks. And now here he was, placing out, as the Reverend had called it, after only a month, and he thought it maybe was not unlike the shipping out his uncle had already done or was about to do. There was a war on—how long had it been off, he wondered—and there was an urgency to things now, no time, it seemed, for detailed explanations of anything. The whole world had become temporary overnight.

Reverend Horton stood at the head of the train and counted heads with one finger. He wrote the number down in a ledger. Ezra counted, too. Forty-seven. Like the blackbirds baked in a pie—no, that had been four and twenty. But here they all were, packed tight, steaming in their little black coats with all the windows closed. It was only a matter of time before they were cooked.

The train lurched and everyone screamed as if it were a roller coaster starting up. Ezra fell against the seat, felt the dizzying pull of the train going backward, watched the platform slide away. Then they were in a tunnel, and the lights in the car flickered as if they weren't strong enough to withstand the dark that pressed against the windows. You could have heard a pin drop except for the steady thunk, thunk of the wheels slowly picking up speed and an unearthly creaking as the train stretched around a curve. Mrs. Worthington was trying to get everyone to sing a hymn—something about crossing over into Jordan. Those who sang, sang timidly. Ezra didn't sing at all. He stared out the window at the dim lights spaced far between in the tunnel. As they passed each one he could see a rock wall behind it. Between the lights, when the window went black again, he could see a startled white face outside the window looking in and it took a minute to realize that that strange face was his own.

The train slowed, stopped. An audible shunting of tracks and then they began to move forward, pulling right. They were under the harbor by now—the walls oozed with water making the black rock slick as coal. They were going faster and the children were singing louder and it seemed it was the singing that moved the train even though he understood it was powered by steam. He didn't know what else to do but sing with them. Maybe God was listening. God, he thought for the first time and not the last, was an orphan, all alone in heaven making up the world, and who was there to praise him except those tiny black specks below rocketing along on a toy train of His own invention?

Ezra's voice had to fight its way out of his throat, cracking as it came. All that half-hearted singing in the dining hall before dinner—now, he thought, we sound like we mean it. This is the sound, he thought, of the heart being torn, this is the sound of wind rushing in. The train broke through the tunnel into the glare of morning in New Jersey. Sky. The sun between trees. And, oh, thank God, blue again.

They stopped singing abruptly as if shocked at what they took to be their own victory, as if they had, in fact, managed to sing their way right out of Hades. There was the world again, after all. How quickly it loomed and receded, rose and fell, buildings ratcheting by. They slowed but sailed right through a small station. As Ezra watched, he saw a man on the platform reading a newspaper, looking up as the train passed. War! the headline said, and the man's face, or half of it, above it like the moon. What did the man think when he saw them—a train of children, round faces pressed to the windows—glory bound, or headed straight for hell? And what moved this man's arm, Ezra asked himself—how did he know it is what we needed—for someone to simply see us and to wave.

A day, a night, another day. Time was marked in increments—so many miles of track and the seconds ticked off by a rhythm that replaced all other sound. Hearts seemed to beat to it, songs, if they were sung, were sung to it—a constant metronome that governed their lives. Ezra had intended to keep to himself—any friendships made would be over at the station coming up or the one after that. There was no point in getting used to anything except the idea that everything was changing. He wrote in his notebook: "Dear Father, the country is bigger than I imagined. Have you ever been to Ohio? Did you know there was a town with my mother's name—Lorain?" He wasn't sure if that was the way it was spelled but he thought his father would be amazed at how well he could write, that he could even write at all, that he had been to school so far almost through the fourth grade and knew how to multiply and divide and that the pyramids in Eypgt contained not only kings and queens but everything on earth they had ever loved and wanted with them when they went to paradise. They were not about to leave anything behind. It would take him a long time, Ezra thought, before he ran out of things to say.

A girl came unsteadily down the aisle, head bent forward and down, like a horse straining against a harness. She tried to balance herself with one hand against the seat backs; in the other she held her suitcase, not by the handle, but pressed against her like a shield. When she raised her head Ezra was shocked to see she had one eye, a black patch where the other had been, and wondered how this had escaped his attention. He'd been trying hard not to miss a thing. Her dark hair hung straight as straw from beneath a green felt cap. She looked to be about twelve years old, though he wondered if the patch somehow didn't make her seem older. She fell against the seat across from him. It had been empty since Lorain when a brother and sister who'd said they'd been specifically requested because they were Lutherans had gotten off and been collectively met by a small congregation. The girl settled herself in the seat, putting the suitcase beside her. With her one eye she looked at Ezra, sizing him up and dismissing him, he felt, with a single glance. She turned and stared for a time out the window. She seemed to soon grow bored with that—it was just green out there, only green—and she turned her attention to her suitcase. She unfastened it carefully as if she didn't quite trust the cardboard to withstand the weight of her hands. She searched through what looked to be a folded nightdress. When her hand emerged it held something Ezra couldn't quite make out— he didn't want to be caught staring—but when she opened her hand and took what lay in her palm between two fingers of her other hand and held it up to the window he could make it out clearly even from across the aisle. A cat's eye marble, its almond-shaped center glowing green inside the clear globe. She put it away again, carefully, and glanced up at him once, a half-smile on her face, as if to let him know that she saw him watching every move she made and didn't mind, had, in fact, counted on his attention and now that she had it, would deliver herself of a few things she had to say. She leaned into the aisle, looked to the front of the car where Mrs. Worthington was handing out jam sandwiches and cups of tea.

"I'm the only girl left," she said. "The other one got off back there but she wasn't hardly more than a baby." Ezra nodded. "They don't want girls—you have to be tiny or ugly to get on this train. Older girls can make their own money, never mind how, but I can tell you they make men pay for kisses—they don't need to go to no farm to wash somebody's clothes for free. I feel sorry for you boys—they'll work you hard—their own sons are in the war now and there's all these fields to plow."

Ezra squirmed in his seat. He didn't want to listen to her any more, but he couldn't stop, either. These were secrets she was telling and she'd deliberately chosen him to tell them to. He wondered if she'd been talking to Irish Danny, too.

"What happened to your eye?" He thought he might as well ask since they were already on such intimate terms.

"I took it out."

He was horrified but he leaned a little closer across the aisle. "On purpose?"

"My glass one—I took it out. I threw it away. I put this patch on—I don't want anyone to take me, I want to get sent back. I will, too. Nobody wants a pirate for a child."

"Did it hurt?" Ezra asked, wincing in advance.

"Not the fake one—the first one—the one that got poked out. I fell on a spindle in a dress factory where I worked—that hurt, though I don't remember exactly how it felt. Anyway," she said, "I can still see with that marble—when I want to."

He had never heard of such a thing but he believed her. When she'd held it up to the light it seemed not like a marble but like something mysterious that might be able to see into the future or at least into the past.

"Will you take it out again?" he asked.

"When it's dark," she said. "It's for seeing in the dark." Like a queen who's uttered a final proclamation she leaned back into the faded red of the once-plush cushion. She closed her one eye. The other, he imagined, stayed perpetually awake and open, looking into the black patch as if it were a screen in a picture show. Elizabeth—he'd seen her name written on her suitcase—Elizabeth's eye simply waited for the cat's eye to open the shutter of night, a gift she obviously did not squander but used judiciously, or only in emergencies. Maybe, he thought, she saw into her life, a little at a time, and so far, nothing of what she saw had frightened her.

The train stopped in Arkansas, in a town near a river. "Not the Arkansas River," Mrs. Worthington had said when he'd asked its name. "I don't know its name but I'm sure it has one."

A small crowd of people were gathered on the platform dressed in black, some holding black umbrellas. They looked like people who had gathered for a funeral train like Lincoln's, Ezra thought, to say goodbye. But they were here to greet and they were prepared for rain though the sun was blindingly bright. He saw that the pavement was wet. Maybe you couldn't trust the sun here for very long. That's something Elizabeth might say, he thought, and smiled to himself at the complicity he already felt as he followed her down the steps. The crowd parted slightly to let them all pass. Elizabeth sauntered down the platform just behind Mrs. Worthington and the Reverend. Ezra thought he could feel the collective dismissal of her by the people who followed behind. She not only had the patch of a pirate, but her saunter probably seemed more like an insolent swagger compared to the slow, sleepy shuffle of the rest.

The Reverend spoke to a man in a dusty top hat who must have been the mayor and they headed up the street. The children followed, suitcases banging against their shins and the townspeople, umbrellas bobbing, throats clearing, were clearly overcome. Maybe one among them had arrived this same way on the first orphan train in 1854, too ashamed to look anyone in the eye. And now here was this haughty girl out front with something close to breasts poking through that terrible coat—what was the world coming to! Ezra, right behind her, for some reason thought of snow, imagined that he was placing his feet exactly in the prints she left behind in soft white powder though her black laced boots left hardly a mark in the hard-baked dirt.

They filed into a hall—a wooden cavern with windows high up. They climbed a set of little stairs to a stage at the front. Mrs. Worthington arranged them, pressing them slightly forward or back to her satisfaction. "Now put your best foot forward," she said. "The right or the left," Ezra whispered to Elizabeth, who let out a huge laugh without filtering it with her hand as most girls were taught to do. Mrs. Worthington emitted a harsh "Shhh!" then said the suitcases should be set down. Shuffling and scraping commenced, magnified by the high-ceilinged room. Through all this the townspeople hardly seemed to breathe. The tension was unbearable. Nobody knew what to do, how to begin. Mrs.

Worthington decided the children should sing and raised her hands, conducting them through the first ragged verse of "Abide with Me" well into the reluctant chorus before her hands fell to her sides and the singing trailed off altogether.

Ezra expected the Reverend to say a prayer, or for the mayor to give some kind of speech, but they seemed like they just wanted to get on with the business at hand. Ezra stole a sideways glance at Elizabeth, who had her arms crossed over her chest. He thought that if she had a watch that this was the moment when she would produce it: flip it open, raise an eyebrow—the one over the patch—at the lateness of the hour, and snap it shut again as if she had somewhere else to be. He looked down at her suitcase and because he knew that the cat's eye was in there he wondered if it could see through the folds of the nightshirt, through the cardboard. He could almost feel it widening as it saw what it saw—the people stepping foward like a dark wave, mounting the stage, emboldened with a purpose. Glasses were put on by those who required them. The inspection began. Arms were felt for muscle or the lack thereof, eyes checked for cauls. A man with hands the size of paddles, the dirt permanently imbedded in the skin, pushed a forefinger into Ezra's mouth and prodded at his teeth. Ezra, nearly choking on the thrust of it, the dirt and sweat, the unbelievable permission of it, shut his eyes tight and bit down hard. The man bellowed and jerked the hand out of Ezra's mouth, held up the finger and shook it at him. "You little dog!" he yelled. Elizabeth laughed, and then, to Ezra's utter astonishment and delight, she actually *barked*, her voice high and clear as a bell breaking through all the murmuring, all attention now turned to her as if she were the cause of the commotion instead of its only appropriate response. Apologies and reprimands from Mrs. Worthington; the two of them were pulled aside. "I know this is difficult, but you're not helping yourselves!" she cried, then sent them back to the line. "What are they going to do," Elizabeth said to Ezra, "send us home?" and she began to laugh again.

The inspection resumed though some were clearly reticent

now. One elderly couple walked arm in arm onto the stage, leaning in a mutual geometry of support. They approached a small boy
who had an obvious limp almost reverently, as if they were on the
threshold of a gift and finally, just inches away, worried that they
might actually be worthy enough to receive it. It was as if the child
himself were choosing them, not the other way around. The three
of them departed, some paper was signed, and they made a different geometry now—the shape of three, the child holding the
woman's hand, the man holding the child's suitcase as if they were
all going home after a long journey together.

The kindness of strangers. The Reverend hadn't been completely wrong. Ezra saw that Elizabeth had been watching the same
three. She wasn't laughing now, she was just looking, and Ezra wondered what exactly it was she saw for her to grow so quiet.

Another child did not go so willingly, but cried pitifully, and
a chain reaction followed. The ones who'd been near tears all along
let go and a flustered Mrs. Worthington tried her best to restore
some sense of composure to the group. She urged them to sing
again but nobody would. One child openly wailed instead. Mrs.
Worthington looked helplessly at Elizabeth, who chose that
moment to stare at the floor. She placed her hands over her ears
and shut her eyes, not, as Ezra thought at first, in annoyance, but
in an attempt to protect herself from something that was drilling
past her bravado right down to her twelve-year-old core. She raised
her head up slowly, her eyes still closed, her ears still covered. She
opened her mouth slowly. Ezra hoped she was going to bark again
but what came out was a sound that stopped the world. Her voice
rose in the cavernous room, up to where the sun scratched against
the windows and dust motes swirled like flecks of brass descending. Elizabeth's voice keened and soared—soprano—singing an aria
in another language altogether. An impossible voice from such a
girl, but there it was, soaring like a swallow that had flown in and
now wanted out. Everybody listened. Nobody wailed, nobody even
breathed until she stopped. The last note of the song spiraled

upward then straight down and flew, it seemed, out the door, back from where it came before it found and inhabited this girl on the bare plank stage of a meeting hall in Arkansas.

"Good Lord," someone said. It was what they all wanted to say.

A pretty young woman stepped forward. She might have had a choir in mind. "I would like to take her," she said gently.

Ezra watched Elizabeth's face—a stricken look on someone long accustomed to guarding her own surprise. She looked as if she knew she had just given herself away.

The young woman leaned close to Mrs. Worthington, who whispered something in her ear. "Elizabeth," the woman called softly. And that did it. The stricken look gave way as an iota of hope fought its way forward. Still, she was divided. Ezra could see it perfectly—a wet streak running down below the patch, her hand swiping at the incriminating evidence; the good eye remained utterly dry.

She picked up her suitcase, then set it down again. She laid it on its side and opened it, kneeling there. She felt for the marble, Ezra knew, and, finding it, held it out to him. "Keep it," she said. "It can tell you where you're going—if you really want to know." She closed the suitcase. She looked up at him. "But if I'd seen this ahead of time, I never would have gotten off the train."

Ezra took the marble. Unless it was held up to the light it didn't look like anything much—a piece of glass you might not even say was green. There wasn't enough light left in the room to change it now. "But if you had seen it," he said, "and you didn't get off the train, then no one would have heard you sing, and she wouldn't have called your name."

"I know," Elizabeth said. "But I don't understand any of it. I don't know what it means." She stood up slowly. The woman was waiting. They walked out of the hall side by side. They did not hold hands. But the woman was speaking to her as they walked, and he could tell by the way that she turned her head that Elizabeth was listening.

When Ezra got on the train again and they pulled out of the station, dusk was a new color—lavender tinged with rust. He thought he saw her once more on the edge of town—two figures in the road, one smaller and striding ahead, the other, taller, pitched forward to keep from getting too far behind. He couldn't tell for sure, but he thought it just like Elizabeth—wherever she was going she was going to get there ahead of time.

He missed her when he looked at the seat she had so briefly occupied. He wondered about how little you had to be around some people to never be able to forget them. They carved themselves right onto your wide open heart, right into your wondering mind. His father—a minute had done it—blood did the rest. But with Elizabeth it was her voice—that wild swallow darting through the eaves that had flown inside him and would not let him sleep. It was a sound he would come to associate with moments, and there would be many in his life, when he felt both free and lost, the way he thought Eve must have felt moving out of Eden, before she had a word for home.

"Dear Father," he wrote. "We are coming into the West. Father, I have never seen so many stars. I believe we will see the Indians soon." He tried to picture his father's face as he wrote, but he was having trouble remembering exactly how his features fit together.

Ezra wrote by match light. One match to a sentence, approximately. They burned at the rate of his thoughts. Sometimes a sentence took more than one match. The last one had taken three. He pressed his face against the window—out there the sky was truly a dome—nothing from horizon to horizon to interrupt the broad reach of the heavens. He tried to count the stars but new ones kept appearing and because they were constantly moving he couldn't tell where they began. For the first time he had a sense of the world turning, of living on something round. He thought there might be fireflies out there though the train was moving too fast to see them. "But if there were fireflies," he wrote, "you wouldn't be able to tell the sky from the ground—everything would be shining." That last sentence took practically all his matches. He'd get some tomorrow at the next stop. A penny for a box of twenty—it made him feel rich to hand over a single coin and get so many of something in return.

Last night they'd slept in a town, on palettes on the floor of a schoolhouse, and had eaten a real supper, but tonight they were on the train to make up for a long delay while the tracks were repaired. He liked being awake when everyone else was asleep—it was easier to think and he could go and stand in the place between the cars where he could feel the wind without anyone coming after him. Two days ago a boy had jumped off when the train stopped to take on water. Reverend Horton wasn't taking any chances. But the Reverend was snoring away—Ezra could hear him from all the way in the back of the car, a saw rasping at the tree of sleep.

Ezra pushed open the door and stepped into the wind that filled that narrow space between cars. He leaned against the gate that closed off the steps. The wind in his face made him squint. He could smell the prairie grass, sweet and dark with dew. He tried to count the stars again—it seemed important to try. He lost his place, started over. At night, alone like this, he imagined himself on a grand adventure whose destination he himself had decided in advance. Los Angeles—City of Angels—it sounded exotic, not like the plain names of so many midwestern towns. He would title his notebook "The Amazing Adventures of Ezra Duvall as Told by Himself." His father would be completely captivated, his full attention won. This kind of thinking was always easier in the dark when the others were asleep and the night stretched out around him, beautiful and infinite. There was room for all the longing he felt— he could send it out without it coming crashing back into the small space inside his head. In these moments he did not feel lonely but believed he contained within him a powerful signal that could be heard. He leaned out farther, over the gate, opened his mouth and howled the way he thought a wolf might, the way Elizabeth surely would; he halfway expected an answer.

He went back to his seat, opened his notebook again. He couldn't, for the moment, think of anything to write. Maybe he would draw a picture instead. He decided to draw his father's face. Painstaking lines, as true to the details as his skill could manage, gathered from a memory four years ago when his father brought him to the rooming house where his uncle lived. That face bending over him in the dark hallway saying he'd be back as soon as he could. Ezra ran out of matches—he'd burned his fingers on the last two.

He drifted off to sleep close to dawn, and when he woke he opened the book to the page he had labored over for so long. It was a face, but it looked like no one that he knew, or had ever known.

"Dear Father," he wrote. "We have been in Texas for days." He held the pencil tightly, point pressed to the page, but nothing else would come. Distinguishing features had deserted the land—the prairie had rolled down to nothing now and what grass there was had been bitten down to dirt by cows. He felt cheated that he hadn't seen any buffalo. The only Indians he'd seen had been hunkered down in the stations in Oklahoma—big, spreading women selling baskets and earthen pots. Some with nothing to sell just waited, watched the children get off, get back on again, herded by a tall, skinny woman in a wilted hat and a short minister who looked too tired to talk to God. Ezra watched the Indians stare at the trains and thought they were waiting in the stations like people still trying to understand the true nature of the enemy who had come to conquer them. Orphans on trains—it probably didn't make any sense to them. Could the families be so weak they could not take them in? The train pulled out and they bent to their baskets once more. Ezra had heard about the Trail of Tears—he'd expected a kind of river, evidence of weeping that the ground would not allow to soak in. He didn't see anything like that, but he felt something like defeat emanating from the ground, rising up and shimmering fitfully like heat lightning, collecting into clouds that would not rain.

The train was nearly empty now. Reverend Horton had gotten off in Denton due to a cable he'd received calling him back to New York and Mrs. Worthington was left in charge of two Italian brothers with a limited vocabulary (the older seemed to be in charge of verbs) and Lars, the Norwegian bully. Technically, she was in charge of Ezra too, but she seemed to have given up on him. She didn't speak to him unless she had to but occasionally she still felt compelled to say, usually after a stop where once again he was not chosen, "You could make more of an effort on your own behalf—no one else can." But he wanted to get all the way out west as long as he was going, not stuck along the way in the middle of nowhere where he'd never be found. He'd developed strategies for getting passed over in these small rural towns. In one, he'd perfected a nervous tic, in another, a fit of coughing. He hadn't had to bite anybody again, but he was prepared to if necessary.

Since he couldn't think of anything to describe in words he thought he'd at least try to draw a landscape. But this part of Texas wasn't giving him much to go on—all he came up with was a single flat horizon line embellished by a solitary cloud.

"What's in your book there?" Lars, the bully, sprawled his Nordic lank over the seat in front of him. There weren't enough boys left to bother, and evidently the Italian brothers weren't worth his time, or maybe between them they'd come up with a convincing comeback. So he'd finally ventured back to Ezra's domain. Ezra sat there as Lars towered over him, acutely aware of the fact that his feet didn't quite reach the floor.

"It's a story," Ezra answered after a long moment of trying to ignore him, a moment in which Lars only leaned closer to peer at the book.

"What kind of story?"

"For my father." He felt a strange thrill at saying those words. "For my father," he said again.

"Your father is alive?" Lars asked. "Then why are you on this train—did he send you away?"

"He is working to get enough money. Then he will come."

Lars raised his pale eyebrows. His eyes were small and hard and not a very nice blue. No wonder he doesn't get picked, Ezra thought.

"That sounds like a story you made up," Lars said.

"It is *not*. It's the *truth*."

"What are you, five years old?"

"I'm *eleven, nearly twelve*."

"Eleven. You're not old enough to know the truth. You only believe what people tell you. I'm sixteen and I know the truth—I was a mistake. I was a mistake but I was not to blame. But you, you are living in a fiction."

"I have proof," Ezra said heatedly, not exactly sure what a fiction was but almost certain he didn't want to live in one. "I have the address where he is." He practically tore his way through the pages to get to the slip of yellow paper. It was not where he had put it. He searched frantically, a page at a time. He upended the book and shook it, he got down on his knees and searched the floor under the seat, around, in front of it—nothing.

Lars got down on the floor to look but didn't put much effort into it. "What did it say?" he asked. "I'll bet you have it memorized—you don't need the piece of paper."

Ezra sat back on his heels. His hands were gray with soot from the floor. "It said Gerald Duvall, see-slash-oh . . ."

"What?"

Ezra wrote it with his finger in the soot on the floor. c/o. "The Pennsylvania Railroad," he said after he'd drawn the symbol.

"Don't you know anything? 'In care of' is not an address. It's not a place."

"He works there—they know who works for them."

"You really believe this?" Lars asked this question almost gently—the meanness gone out of his face and his eyes for a moment were on the blue side of gray. "He's probably in the war by now anyway, not in Pennsylvania. Everyone is going. I will, soon."

Ezra pulled himself back up onto the seat. Of all the thoughts he'd had lately, this was one that hadn't occurred to him. The idea of the war and his father in it and all that could happen or not happen because of it was too big—counting stars was easier. He pulled his knees up so his feet wouldn't dangle. He reached his arms around his knees, one hand holding the other. "I'm not an orphan," he said quietly, more to himself than to Lars.

"But you might as well be," Lars said. He stood up, but unsteadily. The train was rocketing across a trestle bridge. A brown river surged far below. Lars made his way slowly back to the front of the car, looking back over his shoulder more than once along the way as if he thought Ezra might run up and grab him from behind. Ezra put his feet back down. He looked out the window. An enormous cloud of birds passed in front of the sun, darkening it, as if doubt had just crossed the mind of God. Ezra placed the book on his lap and stared at it. What was in it after all but a bunch of words and a picture that didn't add up to much of anything? There was something about Elizabeth's song that had sealed her fate. The canary had sung in the coal mine and lived. Was it safe now to go in? For the first time since he'd gotten on the train he was afraid he'd never get off, that he'd be shunted from town to town, state to state forever until even the stops disappeared and he was on the straight and endless horizon, a ruler laid out to the end of his life, the sun moving in a circle, horizontally instead of up and down day after endless day without division and the moon never getting a chance to shine. He took Elizabeth's marble out of his pocket where he'd kept it safe and held it up to the window, brought his eye up to it and looked. The world bent down, out of its infinite width and breadth and was for a moment contained inside a green corona. At that moment everything, the dust and soot on the seatcushion, the yellow light that fell equally on the dark heads of the Italian brothers, the hills that were rising from the ground again, the water tower in the distance that meant a town, a horse that had to be coaxed, pulled forward by a girl to step out of its traces near a barn just outside of town, even a man folding a newspaper just as the train was coming into the station— Kerrville, the wooden sign behind him said—all of these things were so vivid and fragile he was afraid if he did not write them down they would disappear.

He didn't see the future anywhere inside Elizabeth's green eye. He couldn't clearly see the man who had folded the newspaper— how he would become his next father within an hour, how he, Ezra Duvall, would let himself be chosen. He couldn't have predicted how later, much later, the man would say he'd chosen him because of the notebook, that he had not come to the station for anyone that afternoon. But he had seen him on the platform, writing, and was moved in ways he never would have imagined, by a child who came from nothing and found so much to say.

Photograph by Phil Lancaster

About the Author

Alison Moore is a former assistant professor of English/Creative Writing in the MFA Creative Writing Program at the University of Arizona and a current Humanities Scholar in Arkansas. She received her MFA from the Warren Wilson Program for Writers in 1990. Currently, she lives in Fayetteville, Arkansas, and Terlingua, Texas, and is completing a novel on the Orphan Trains. She has developed public outreach programs for the Orphan Train Heritage Society of America, Inc., and for ArtsReach, a Native American literacy project in southern Arizona. She is the author of two books, a collection of short stories entitled *Small Spaces between Emergencies* (Mercury House, 1992) one of the Notable Books of 1993 chosen by the American Library Association, and a novel, *Synonym for Love* (Mercury House, 1995). She has received several national awards as well as state arts council awards and was the winner of the Katherine Ann Porter Prize for Fiction in 2004. Alison and her husband, musician Phil Lancaster, have been touring Arkansas, Texas, and Arizona performing a multimedia program about the Orphan Trains with funding from state Humanities Councils. For more info about this program and others, visit the web site: www.extraordinarystories.org

195